"Abby, what do you really have to lose?"

Colin went on. "I don't know for sure how this last week felt to you, but for me, it hurts like hell to feel like I'm on the outside of your life, looking in."

"I'm just trying to—"

"To protect yourself," he finished before she could. "We have so much history, Abby. To ignore what we feel…it's just impossible. I'm not asking you to go to bed with me—not until we're both sure of our feelings."

Abby hesitated.

"I'd be good to you, Abby," Colin whispered. "Come on. Give us a chance."

Abby focused on Colin as he watched his daughter. He wore the open, loving smile reserved for Jessie. And she had to wonder where she'd ever find a man more *worthy* of a second chance….

Dear Reader,

For Jessie's Sake is the last installment in the Hopewell Vineyard series, and I find myself reluctant to say goodbye. Hopetown doesn't exist only in my mind. It's the actual site of a vineyard outside New Hope, Pennsylvania. It sits high above a river at the end of a twisting road. And there is a historic homestead along that road that was the inspiration for Hopewell Manor. Sadly, the real town and many others along the river are facing the same flood threat as my Hopetown.

This final book explores the far-reaching effects of lies and follows the struggles of Abby, the youngest Hopewell sister, and Colin, the man she grew up adoring but who broke her teenaged heart. Together they must unravel the web of deceit woven long ago by two men—one who loved to wield power and another whose greed sought such power. And when Abby and Colin do, they will discover that true love really does conquer all.

Enjoy,

Kate Welsh

FOR JESSIE'S SAKE

KATE WELSH

Silhouette®
SPECIAL EDITION®
Published by Silhouette Books
America's Publisher of Contemporary Romance

ISBN-13: 978-0-373-24878-0
ISBN-10: 0-373-24878-4

FOR JESSIE'S SAKE

This edition published by arrangement with Harlequin Books S.A.

Visit Silhouette Books at www.eHarlequin.com

Printed in U.S.A.

Books by Kate Welsh

Silhouette Special Edition

Substitute Daddy #1542
The Doctor's Secret Child #1734
A Bargain Called Marriage #1839
For Jessie's Sake #1878

Steeple Hill Love Inspired

For the Sake of Her Child #39
Never Lie to an Angel #69
A Family for Christmas #83
Small-Town Dreams #100
Their Forever Love #120
**The Girl Next Door* #156
**Silver Lining* #173
**Mountain Laurel* #187
**Her Perfect Match* #196
Home to Safe Harbor #213
**A Love Beyond* #218
**Abiding Love* #252
**Autumn Promises* #265
Redeeming Travis #271
Joy in His Heart #325

*Laurel Glen

KATE WELSH

is a two-time winner of Romance Writers of America's coveted Golden Heart Award and was a finalist for the RITA® Award in 1999. Kate lives in Havertown, Pennsylvania, with her husband of over thirty years. When not at work in her home office, creating stories and the characters that populate them, Kate fills her time in other creative outlets. There are few crafts she hasn't tried at least once or a sewing project that hasn't been a delicious temptation. Those ideas she can't resist grace her home or those of friends and family.

As a child she often lost herself in creating make-believe worlds and happily-ever-after tales. Kate turned back to creating happy endings when her husband challenged her to write down the stories in her head. Her goal is to entertain her readers with wholesome stories of romantic love.

Acknowledgment

I would like to thank everyone
at Sand Castle Winery, especially Joseph,
for their invaluable information and
lovely winery and vineyard. Without your vision,
mine would never have been born.

Dedication

Daddy,

You lived your final days as I wrote this book, ever unselfish, always gracious. You showed me so much just by the way you lived your life. You are my first hero and some of you lives in every hero I create. You taught me what a man should be, how a husband should love, how a father should protect, teach and nurture. You showed me that a legacy happens only by a life well lived. You told everyone who visited in those last years that you were the happiest man in the world—and you meant it. You always told us if you stood on the top of a mountain and looked back at your life, at every fork in the road, you'd know you'd made the right choice. I don't know if I'll be able to say that at the end of my life, but I do know I started on my road from the best place anyone could—from your loving arms. You will be forever missed. There will never be another like you because the Lord broke the mold the day you were born. I will be forever grateful that you were here for me and with me for so long.

Tatter

Chapter One

Colin McCarthy had returned to Hopetown, and Abby Hopewell's world had tilted off its axis.

Life as she'd known it—as she'd carefully recreated it—had just ended in a flash of thunder and lightning.

He stood in Cliff Walk's gleaming foyer, dripping on her carefully restored hardwood floors. Worse, he still looked every bit as gorgeous as the last time she'd seen him.

Same thick mane of mahogany-colored hair. Same stormy blue eyes. She still felt the same electricity just being in his presence, the overwhelming need to feel his arms around her.

She clenched a fist under her desk. He was still the

same man who'd become her first and only lover, then turned into a coldhearted stranger within minutes.

"Abby," Colin said, and stared, clearly as shocked to see her as she was to see him. For a moment, his expression was gentle and loving, then hot and hungry the way it had been that one time…but then his lips tightened, his jaw hardened. His eyes went glacial. "What's an illustrious Hopewell doing working as a desk clerk in a backwater bed-and-breakfast?"

The change puzzled her now as much as it had then. She'd done nothing but admit to loving him. Nothing but give him all she was—all she had to give. He was the one who'd changed. Who'd hurt *her.*

Nevertheless, hearing the tone in his voice tore her heart in two all over again, reminding her of the most painful moments of her life.

She'd stepped out of Colin's bedroom that long-ago night they'd made love, still feeling cherished yet prepared for a bit of awkwardness. That would have made sense. What she hadn't been ready for was Colin's harsh dismissal of her and the feelings she'd thought they shared.

Abby had spent years rehearsing for this moment but, by showing up on her doorstep out of the blue, he'd taken her by surprise. She reached inside herself, searching for the calm she desperately needed, clearing her senses of the longing he'd always made her feel.

She wasn't less nervous but she *was* in control, her tone cool and collected. She said in her frostiest tone, "Cliff Walk is actually a very successful and highly acclaimed establishment. And since I happen to be part owner and manager here," she went on, her voice managing somehow to chill even further, "I have the right to ask you to remove yourself from the premises. Good night."

The Hopewells didn't have the money they'd had before her father's death and the subsequent lawsuit that had all but bankrupted his estate. But they were no longer so badly off financially that she had to put up with having someone so detestable under her roof.

She looked back down at the receipts she'd carefully sorted. They'd been stirred like leaves in a hurricane when Colin had opened the door. With an annoyed huff Abby began resorting her piles, pretending his presence was of little consequence. She hoped he didn't notice the way her hands shook.

Then a small voice brightened the stormy night while making Abby's heart ache. "Oh, Daddy! I was right. It *is* a palace. And you bringed me to meet Snow White!"

Abby looked up to see a tiny cherub about four years old clinging to Colin's leg under his dripping slicker. Without warning, the child broke away and zipped across the foyer to the Victorian desk where Abby sat rooted to her chair.

The little girl wore an expression of complete and total awe. Like Abby, she had pitch-black shoulder-length hair, but hers looked as if it hadn't seen a comb in a week. Unlike Abby, who'd often cursed her fair skin, the child had a soft olive complexion that happened to be smeared with some undeterminated food. She had big, deep brown, nearly-black eyes—the left sporting a genuine black eye. Right then they were wide and adoring as she stared at Abby. The child's clothes were rumpled, spotted with raindrops and more suited to a boy than a girl.

She was adorable.

And had her father not turned out to be the scum of the earth, she might have been Abby's child. The night of Abby's high school graduation had caused her so much grief that nine years later she still loathed the entire month of June.

And, of course, Colin McCarthy.

"Do you live in this palace?" Colin's daughter asked, still apparently confusing Abby with a fairy-tale character.

Colin advanced and put his hands protectively on the child's shoulders. "The lady just runs this bed-and-breakfast, Jessie. She lives in a big fancy house by the river."

"Actually, I *do* live here," Abby told the child, only too happy to contradict her father. "That way if a guest needs me for something in the middle of the night, I'm available. The house your daddy was talking about is Hopewell Manor. It's where I grew up and it's about half a mile up the road from Torthúil. That makes us neighbors."

The little cherub crossed her arms. "Daddy says Torhool," she pronounced carefully, "is a Irish word. Right, Daddy?"

Colin nodded, still hovering.

Jessie McCarthy was simply darling. Abby fought a grin as a new pain stabbed her heart. If there was a child, there was a mother? A wife.

Abby glanced at the door, but no one had followed them inside. So where was she?

"Torthúil mean *fruitful*," Jessie said, grabbing Abby's attention again.

"And when it was a farm it certainly was fruitful," Abby agreed. "I used to walk down the road to buy pints of strawberries from your grandparents. Blackberries, too. Sometimes I'd get a nice crisp apple or peach to eat on my way home." Memories flowed from her tongue, and she hoped Colin hadn't noticed. In those days catching even a glimpse of him had been half the reason for the long walks.

And she'd told him so that fateful June night.

"I don't like it there," Jessie declared. "It's a creepy house. I want to stay here. Then I can be a princess, like you."

"I'm not really a princess," Abby protested.

"That's not the way I remember it," Colin muttered.

Abby glared at him. Honestly, you'd think she was the one who'd hurt him and not the other way around. Not only had he cruelly dismissed her after she'd given him her body—and her love—he'd cost Abby her friendship, with his sister, Tracy.

Colin's parents must have found out about that night—they'd probably overheard him talking to his friend, Harley Bryant, lying about how she'd offered herself to him and he'd turned her down. Whatever had happened, his parents had forbidden Tracy to be in Abby's company ever again. Losing her closest friend had been devastating enough, but the rift had also set Tracy on a downward spiral that had killed her within months. Colin hadn't been able to come home for Tracy's funeral and so had robbed Abby of the opportunity to tell him his sister's death was his fault.

Abby wanted badly to tell Colin what she thought of him right then and there, but didn't want to upset his sweet child. Besides, she was no longer sure she wanted him to know how much past events still haunted her. She didn't want him to have the satisfaction.

Colin stooped down to eye level with Jessie. "Kitten, why don't you go explore that room in there," he said, pointing toward the parlor. "But don't touch anything. Okay?"

"Okay," she sang out as she went to explore.

Colin watched her go, then turned to Abby. "I didn't know the house had fallen into such disrepair or I would have made other arrangements."

She'd liked his father and felt it only right to acknowledge his passing. "Before you go further, I was sorry to hear about your father. He was a good man."

He nodded. "I'm sorry for your loss, too. My father's death is part of why I came back to take possession of Torthùil. But it's not safe to stay there with Jessie. We could go into town but—" A loud clap of thunder and a bright flash of lightning lit up the foyer, Jessie shrieked in fear as she ran back to her father's waiting arms. Colin scooped her up and held her tight. "It's okay, Jess. I've got you."

Abby stared at them for a long moment, remembering how it felt to be held in those arms in a very different type of embrace. Then Colin's gaze returned to her and Abby snapped out of it, looking away.

As angry as she was, Abby couldn't send a child back out into the storm. There were bed-and-breakfasts along the road leading to Hopetown, but her brother-in-law had already called to warn her how dangerous the road was tonight. The look in Colin's eyes said he was well aware of the deteriorating conditions.

Abby sighed in defeat. "I wouldn't send a dog out into this weather and certainly not a couple with a child. Is your wife in the car?"

Abby's question took Colin by surprise. All his friends in L.A. and, of course, his family knew the story of his inconvenient marriage. He and Jessie had been on their own for so long that he'd forgotten most people would assume Jessie had a mother in her life.

"It's just Jessie and me. We're McCarthy and Daughter, right, partner?" he said and gave the child a short, affectionate squeeze.

Jessie, fright forgotten for the moment, pulled her head off his shoulder to kiss him on the cheek. Her smile stretched from ear to ear when she looked back at Abby and nodded vigorously. "Daddy and me am partners. We do everyfing togever."

Abby stared for a long moment then nodded. "I have a room with twin beds." She smiled at Jessie. "I don't imagine Jessie wants to be far from her partner on a night like this."

Colin frowned. "If you could show us to the room, I'll get Jessie settled, then go back out to the truck for our things."

"And leave her all alone in your room?" She shook her head. "Go now. I can keep an eye on her here."

Colin hesitated. Even though Jessie was squirming to get down again so she could talk to "Snow," he wasn't sure he was comfortable leaving Abby with his child.

Abby sighed. "Oh, for heaven's sake, she'll be perfectly safe here with me."

He thought about it then gave her a quick nod. "Fine. I won't be more than a minute or two." He set Jessie down and rushed back out into the deluge. As he reached the edge of the perfectly restored Victorian's porch, the sky lit up once again. He blinked. In the distance he would swear he'd seen what looked like a Tuscan village. On the next flash, row after row of grapevines blinked into view before the dark of night returned to hide them.

What on earth had this place become?

A deafening clap of thunder reminded him of his mission. Without further delay, Colin ducked his head and ran out into the torrential rain. He jumped into the cab of the truck in an effort to stay just a bit drier while gathering up their things. He reached back and pulled the overnight luggage from the backseat then noticed Jessie's toys and her precious stuffed dog abandoned on the floor. He grinned as he picked it up. *Can't leave you behind, Dog-dog.*

Jessie had been just shy of eleven months old when one of his sisters sent the stuffed animal for Christmas. Jessie had seen it under the tree and said "Dog-dog"—her first words after "Da-da." The toy had been her constant companion since. Colin didn't know if that was because Angelina had walked out of their lives for good around the time the toy arrived. Because of her attachment to Dog-dog, Colin worried constantly that there was a void in Jessie's life that he'd failed to fill.

He'd married Angelina when she'd learned she was pregnant. The condom had failed and she'd been bitter about her pregnancy and the disruption of her acting career. Luckily he'd been able to appeal to her strict Catholic upbringing to convince her to carry the baby to term.

Angelina had married him for legal and insurance purposes only. They'd never lived together as man and wife. She had visited Jess sporadically for nearly a year, but then she'd decided to cut all ties to them and return to her native Brazil where stardom and a television series awaited.

Jessie had been his and his alone from the day she'd gone home from the hospital with Colin, and they'd been inseparable since. He chuckled as he stuffed her other toys into his bag and thought back to the looks he'd gotten when he'd shown up on the construction site the next workday after he brought her home. He'd had Jessie and a young nanny in the pickup's cab and had parked a dilapidated construction trailer out front where they'd spend their days. The trailer had looked pretty bad, but he'd renovated and sanitized the inside within an inch of its remaining lifespan and had turned it into a traveling nursery.

The guys had all stood staring at him as if he'd lost his mind, but he'd taken Jess and that trailer to every house he'd renovated or flipped since. It had been her home away from home until just last week. She really was his partner. And she had more than fifty honorary aunts and uncles from his crews.

But she'd never really had a mother.

Lightning struck again, reminding him that she did have a father and she was probably missing him. Tucking Dog-dog inside his raincoat, Colin gathered up the luggage—one old UCLA gym bag and one brandnew Snow White rolling suitcase.

Snow White, he thought with gritted teeth as he ran for the front porch again. He'd had the same reaction to Abby the first day he'd become aware of the little girl growing up on the property next to Torthúil. She'd been farther upstream with her family on a picnic. The current had caught her inner tube and carried her away from them. She'd been unconcerned and laughing happily when he'd fished her out of the river near Torthúil's levee. And the resemblance to the fairy-tale princess had only strengthened as she'd grown.

She'd truly looked the part by the time she'd hit her

teenage years. It was about then that he'd realized his affection for his sister's friend had grown into something more. Much more. He'd known she was too young for him and had enlisted in the army as soon as he graduated high school that next summer, hoping to put distance between them.

But as predicted by an old saying of his mother's, absence had really made his heart grow fonder or he'd never have weakened four years later when he'd come home for his sister Tracy's graduation. It had been Abby's graduation, too. He'd thought Abby was still as innocent as her fairy-tale alter ego that day. But he'd been wrong. She had turned into a seductress in his absence.

Colin entered the lobby and froze in place. Jessie sat on the step below Abby happily having her hair combed, which was nothing short of a miracle since that really meant having it untangled. It was one of the few bones of contention between them. She didn't want it cut short, but she didn't want the tangles combed out, either.

"When we get this done, we'll braid it," Abby told Jessie. "If you wear it to bed braided, it won't tangle as much. A satin pillowcase usually helps, too. I'll give your daddy one to put on your pillow tonight. And there's a rinse in your bathroom to help keep it silky so it tangles less to begin with. There. Now we braid it," she said, drawing out the syllables as her fingers flew through Jessie's hair, deftly doing as she'd promised. In seconds she was tying off a smooth sleek braid that hung down his daughter's back.

"And now it's done," Abby went on. "Okay, hair combed and braided, hands and face washed. Looks like all you have left is to get your pj's on and brush your teeth, and have your bedtime snack!"

"I even get a snack?" Jessie said with dreamy wonder. "Are you sure this isn't a palace? What kind of cookies you have?"

After his thoughts in the car, seeing Abigail Hopewell attending his child so lovingly nearly took him to his knees. Jessie's own mother had never shown her the easy kind of affection Abby seemed to dole out so naturally. Then he remembered what she'd done to *him* and he realized he shouldn't let her within a country mile of his child. If it weren't for his worry for Jessie at Torthúil, he'd whisk her out of here so fast Abby would barely see his dust.

"Well, let's see. I think Genevieve made shortbread. And we always have lots of milk, of course," she was saying to Jessie.

"Jessie's allergic to milk," he growled.

Jessie frowned, clearly wondering what was wrong with him since she rarely heard that tone of voice. At the same time Abby's gaze snapped from him to Jessie with alarm. "I'm so sorry, sweetie, I had no idea but it's okay, I have soy milk, too. Do you like that?"

"Uh-huh. Can I have some, Daddy?"

It was small of him, but Jessie looked so hopeful about having a treat—and if he wasn't wrong, some more time with Abby—that he felt left out. He was Jessie's hero and he wanted it to stay that way. "Sure, partner," he said as cheerfully as he could manage. "But there's someone here who was pretty scared out in the car. I'll bet she'd like to have some hugs from her person." He pulled out her stuffed companion.

"Dog-dog!" Jessie shrieked and ran to him, warming Colin's heart with her grateful smile.

Abby stood, too, her face blank. Her tone became chilly. "I'll bring her snack to your room. If you wouldn't mind finding it on your own, it's at the top of the stairs to the left. Number Ten." She handed him the key and when their hands brushed he felt the familiar traitorous surge of raw need rush through him, something he remembered from all those years ago. And unless Colin missed his guess when Abby's eyes flew to his, she'd felt it, too.

Colin snatched his hand back and frowned. This wouldn't do. He had reasons for returning and Abby had nothing to do with them. "We can find it on our own," he assured her. And once there he'd bolt the door against all she was still able to make him feel. "About the snack, we wouldn't want to put you out. Jessie doesn't need one. I'm sure you aren't in the habit of playing waitress."

Abby arched one of her finely shaped eyebrows. Her emerald eyes had gone as hard as stone, telling him that though she felt the same attraction she once had she didn't want feelings for him, either. "Actually, I often cater to my guests. It's my job. And I love it. I'll be up with Jessie's snack in a few minutes. Oh, and there's an en suite bathroom in your room so you won't need to worry that Jessie will wander in the middle of the night."

Colin watched her go, childishly tempted to stick his tongue out at her retreating back. He raked a hand through his hair. Dear God, he'd lost at least five hundred points off the maturity scale since walking in the front door. Why was he letting her do this to him?

Because she's always done things to you. That's what caused all the trouble in the first place. She's never even needed to try.

"She isn't Snow White, you know," Jessie said, her voice full of awe. "But isn't she won'erful?"

Colin could think of plenty of other words, but he tried to keep his tone calm for Jessie. "Let's get you upstairs and ready for bed," he all but growled.

And then he'd figure out a way to rid himself of the still-powerful attraction he apparently felt for Abby. Once and for all.

Chapter Two

Abby set the glass of vanilla-flavored soy milk and a plate of cookies on the tray, then added the crystal bud vase and the rose she'd picked earlier to save it from the approaching storm. She surveyed her work and nodded in approval. She wanted the evening to be special for Jessie since Torthúil had been such a disappointment to her. Besides, she thought every little girl should feel like a princess at least once in her life.

She smiled, remembering when she and her sisters were that age. All those magical bedtime rituals—snacks and stories, kisses and special toys. They always had their mother *and* Hannah Canton, their ever-faithful and affectionate housekeeper, fussing over them. Apparently Jessie had no one but a father who clearly didn't even know how to avoid tangles in her hair.

With that thought fresh in her mind, Abby stopped as she passed the linen closet. She pulled down the satin pillowcase she'd mentioned and tucked it under her arm before moving like a rusted tin soldier toward the end of the hall.

She stood frozen at the door to Number Ten, afraid to face Colin again. What was the matter with her? This nervousness was a far cry from the righteous anger she wanted to feel. Should feel. In spite of what he'd done, this was attraction. Dangerous attraction. Her unwavering love for him hadn't faded even after he'd rejected her so cruelly in front of his friend. Abby had held out hope that he'd arrive at Hopewell Manor to tell her he'd been trying to protect her reputation from Harley's wagging tongue. But when she'd learned he'd left town ahead of schedule, Abby had buried her foolish, passionate dreams.

She'd forced herself to date two other men since that awful night. One had been a political science major in her sophomore year of college, the other a hotel manager who'd stayed at Cliff Walk during the first Hopetown Arts Festival a couple of years ago.

She'd been marginally attracted to both of them and tried to take both relationships to the next level, but she'd always frozen, instinctively pulling back when things got physical. When she'd asked for more time, neither had taken her request well. Both had cruelly dismissed her needs. Finally she'd decided to act as cold and remote as they'd accused her of being. Fear of making another mistake, of trusting her own judgment, had simply paralyzed her.

She'd learned her lesson not once but three times—she just wasn't cut out for romance. Passion was an unruly, dangerous emotion, and she wasn't willing to risk her heart again. So she'd carefully built a quiet, secure life for herself.

So what if some people thought it was too quiet. Too sterile. So what if she'd been called an ice queen by her ex-boyfriends? So what if the title now fit. It was comfortable.

Safe.

Abby stiffened her spine, refusing to dither any longer. Checking her expression in the hall mirror, she was gratified to find a cool look firmly in place. Colin could never know what he made her feel. He'd gloat or try to take advantage of it.

She took a deep breath. Ready to see him, she rapped on the door. As it swung open, Abby's heart started thundering behind her ribs, but it was Jessie who answered. "Hi. Daddy's gettin' changed on account of he says he's wet through his Skivvies. Is that my snack?"

Abby blinked away the flash of Colin sans Skivvies. "Y-yes," she stammered, trying to drag her mind off that disturbing enticing vision. "And here's the pillowcase I promised you."

Jessie sucked in a deep breath, a sweet little gasp of awe and gratitude. Then she took the pillowcase and ran it across her cheek. "Oh, Miss Abby. So soft and silky."

Abby smiled. "That's why it works. Your hair will just slide over it and not tangle."

The door to the bathroom flew open at the moment Jessie charged into her arms, wrapping her in an exuberant hug. Abby managed to steady the tray as Colin asked, "Jessie, who are you—" He froze in the doorway, frowning.

Abby could only stare. He was bare chested. His jeans were zipped, but the button was undone and he had a towel tossed over one strong, muscular shoulder. He still had those damned six-pack abs.

With loose-limbed grace, he walked toward her and reached for the tray. When his fingers made contact with hers, Abby jerked her hands away, nearly upsetting the glass. "I—I'm s-sorry." She backed away toward the door. "I hope you like your snack, Jessie. Breakfast is at nine. Enjoy your stay at Cliff Walk."

She made it to the hall and pulled the door closed. Heart pounding, she rested her forehead on the cool door and took a deep, calming breath. She had to get hold of herself. She couldn't let his mere presence rattle her like this. He was nothing more than a rat in men's clothing. Very little clothing to be sure, but a rat was a rat. No matter what he did or didn't wear.

No matter what he did to her senses.

Determined to find her center and calm her troubled mind, Abby closed up her house for the night and retreated to the tower room. It had once been the maid's room, but now it was her retreat. She stopped at the top of the stairs, waiting for the familiar sense of peace the place always brought her, but instead of feeling the comforting shelter the space usually gave her, an oppressive loneliness seemed to descend on her. Everyone in her life had someone but her. When she was upset her refuge was a place, not a person.

But that was the way she wanted it, she reminded herself. That was the way it had to be. Rather than wallow, she yanked at the buttons of her blouse and moved toward her dresser. It was simply the turbulent weather working on her. Or the shock of seeing Colin again.

Or maybe it was nothing more than the rapidly fading feeling of Jessie's grateful hug. Or Colin's touch.

Shaking herself loose of her useless observations, Abby stripped out of her clothes and got into her leotard. Then she sank to the yoga mat in front of the tall Victorian windows. After a deep cleansing breath, she moved into her first position, ignoring the flashes of lightning, the rumble and crack of the thunder, and sought her center—her peace.

An hour later she had twisted and stretched into every yoga position she'd mastered and had tried a few she hadn't. Fresh from a shower, she climbed into bed and acknowledged the truth.

The past still haunted her.

She told herself that other than having a father who expected his children to earn his love, her early life had gone along just fine. All the trouble and turmoil had really started when she'd decided to stay at Tracy's house on graduation night nine years ago.

She'd just turned out the light in Torthùil's kitchen after washing the few dishes from her midnight snack when Colin's voice had drifted in the back screen door of the McCarthys' farmhouse.

Abby had loved Colin with all her heart and soul for years and had grown tired of being ignored and treated like a little girl. So she'd adopted what she'd hoped was a sexy stance, hoping he'd realize she really had grown up in his absence.

She'd called his name in her best Marilyn Monroe "Happy Birthday, Mr. President" voice and hope had stirred in her heart when her soldier boy seemed nervous. So she'd stood on tiptoe and brought her lips within inches of his.

To his credit he'd tried to warn her off after a hearty gulp of air, but it had been too late. She'd tasted victory. So she'd run her index finger down his chest and across those sexy abs. And passion had exploded between them…

Abby sprang up in bed. The storm raged outside her snug tower lair, but she was soaked to the skin. Soaked in sweat. She'd gone back to where she'd sworn she'd never go.

And all because Colin McCarthy was under her roof.

Colin sat in the chair by the window watching Jessie sleep. He didn't have that luxury. Seeing Abby again had brought back memories of the painful series of incidents that had been a huge turning point in his life.

And what about her life?

She seemed so very different. Yet with Jessie, she was as sweet and kind as he remembered her being with his younger sisters. Abby had always worn a smile. Her eyes had always shone with joy. She'd been a little impish, with a verve for life that had always made him pause and see the enjoyment in the simplest things when she was around the McCarthy house—which was often.

It was the new coolness in her eyes that shocked him, almost as much as her presence at the B and B. The last time he'd seen those eyes they'd been filled with hurt and tears. He closed his own now, trying to forget what had caused the tears, and the price he'd been forced to pay for them the next day.

When that didn't work, he realized he needed to do something he'd been avoiding since his decision to return to Hopetown. He needed to reexamine his part in the mess that had followed those stolen moments with Abby in his bed. Colin forced himself to examine how he'd handled his mistake.

The moment his mind had cleared of the effect of maybe one too many beers and Abby's scent, the consequences of what they'd done had crashed in on him like a ten-ton weight.

Colin had felt panic rise just as he had the out-of-control desire not long before. She was still a kid who didn't seem to see the mess they could have caused. First, he hadn't used protection and she'd clearly been a virgin. They both had years of school left. And he'd also belatedly remembered he'd been lying with her naked in his arms and his room had barely been more than a converted porch off his parent's kitchen!

When Harley Bryant walked into the kitchen, he'd jumped up and tossed his clothes on, ordering Abby to do the same. Harley Bryant had had the biggest mouth in two counties. Colin had stepped into the kitchen pulling the door shut behind him, assuming Abby would stay hidden, but she hadn't. Harley had figured out what had happened, so Colin denied it. But he'd done it clumsily. If Abby had so much as touched him, she would have confirmed Harley's suspicions and the whole town would've known. So the best he could do was to sneer that she was so young that her having made a pass at him was a joke. Then he'd coldly sent her off to bed.

God, he'd been such a damned clod. He should have found a better way to disarm the situation than being so cruel to her. And he had been cruel. In trying to protect her, he'd hurt her more than gossip ever could have.

Lightning lit the sky outside the tall window in the front room at Cliff Walk at the same moment thunder cracked and literally rattled the windowpanes. Jessie sat up and screamed before Colin could make it to the bed. "It's okay, honey. Daddy's here."

He settled on the bed facing her and Jessie covered

her ears as another clap rolled overhead. "It's so loud. I don't like it."

Colin scooped her up into his lap and snuggled her head under his chin. "It always helps me to remember that thunder can't hurt anyone. It's just the clouds banging together."

Jessie yawned expansively. "Well, I wish they'd stop it."

"Me, too," he admitted. He turned so his back was against the headboard, still cuddling Jessie to his chest. He rubbed her back, trying to soothe her fears. "Try to sleep. Daddy'll hold you till the storm passes, and tomorrow we'll get started on our house. Once the repairs are done, you can help me pick the colors of the rooms." He smiled in the dark. "You're going to like it here. I promise."

Jessie yawned. "Brown like my magic rock. I want the house to match my rock," she told him then dropped off to sleep. He smiled a little sadly remembering when, like Jessie, he'd thought a daddy could fix anything. But he knew that, like his father before him, there were a lot of things he and Jessie's "magic rock" couldn't fix.

He'd picked up the rock she treasured on the morning he'd left Torthúil—all but run out of town on a rail by James Hopewell. He'd kept it to remind him of the home he'd lost so he'd never stop fighting to be as rich and powerful as the man who'd forced him to leave. That day he hadn't been sure he'd ever see Torthúil again. He'd given the rock to Jessie when he'd known they would be returning because the closer the move to Pennsylvania got, the more anxious she'd grown of the changes to come.

And it was the things neither he nor the "magic rock" could fix—his own guilt and his anger at Abby—that were keeping him awake.

As he sat there nine years later, holding Jessie in his arms, revisiting what had happened that morning so long ago, things looked different. James Hopewell's anger toward Colin looked different. Wouldn't Colin go to nearly any length to protect Jessie? So, okay, maybe Hopewell showing up at Torthúil the next day was understandable. He'd still been shepherding two of his daughters through their teenage years, so having expected Colin's parents to be involved in the meeting made sense. As was telling Colin to get out of town, to stay out so he and Abby had no further contact. That, too, fell in the forgivable range.

But the rest of what Hopewell had done was still simply unforgivable and inexcusable. He had threatened to see to it that the local bank foreclosed on the McCarthy's farm if Colin didn't agree to all his demands. Because their loan had been slightly delinquent and because Hopewell was powerful enough to make good on the threat, Colin had known it was a real possibility. And if Abby had turned up pregnant, nothing would have saved his family from her father's wrath.

Then later that summer Hopewell had crossed the line into cruelty by refusing to allow Colin to return to Hopetown for his younger sister's funeral.

Some would say Hopewell had done him a favor, and Colin acknowledged that it was probably true. He'd made Colin so angry that he'd worked like a Trojan to achieve the success he'd desired. But Abby had betrayed him by telling her father what had happened.

He hadn't believed she'd gone to her father, had nearly denied the truth until Hopewell went on to explain that he'd met Abby when she'd come in that morning. She'd been crying, he said, so he'd comforted her, then pressed her for the truth until she confessed everything. Nothing would have convinced Colin to betray Abby but, he sighed, she *had* been young. Immature. Now that he'd seen her all grown-up, that fact was pretty hard to ignore, and harder to hold against her.

But there was still Tracy's death and the belief he'd long harbored in his heart, that Abby had somehow played a part in his sister's death. How else would Tracy have met the rich kid who'd been drunk behind the wheel of the boat the day she was killed? He'd no doubt been a member of the privileged crowd the Hopewells hung around with.

Well, James Hopewell was dead now. And that left Colin with a problem. What did he do with not just his anger toward Hopewell for his ill treatment but with this powerful attraction to the man's daughter?

Chapter Three

Abby peeked around the kitchen door into Cliff Walk's dining room. Her ace chef, Genevieve Richards, had prepared the meals each guest had requested the night before and now everyone sat happily eating. Everyone but Colin and his adorable child. Abby had been so knocked off her stride last night that she'd forgotten to ask them to choose from the selections on the breakfast menu. Consequently Genevieve hadn't even known they'd checked in.

"All set, Abby," Genevieve said from right next to her.

Abby jumped a mile, nearly upsetting the tray in her chef's hand.

"Oh, God, Genevieve," she gasped. "Don't sneak up on me like that."

Genevieve looked down at her generous waistline and chuckled. "I'm too heavy on my feet to sneak anywhere and you know it."

"Then what were you doing right there next to me?" Abby demanded.

She was immensely fond of her chubby cook who always joked about her weight and her unrepentant love of food. So when Genevieve looked at her as if she'd lost her mind, Abby wasn't about to argue the point since she was nearly sure she had.

"I was on my way into the dining room to serve the last of the meals. You were in my way," Genevieve explained patiently.

Abby felt a blush color her cheeks. "Sorry. I was preoccupied."

"You sure are interested in that hunk out there. Why aren't you in there chatting with him and your other guests the way you usually do?"

"Interested? Me? Don't be silly. I loathe the man." She refused to comment on her neglect of the guests. The way Genevieve was staring at her, Abby already felt like a bug under a microscope, so she didn't intend to give her friend more ammunition.

"Any woman who'd loathe a man who looks like that and treats his kid like she's the center of his universe needs to have her head examined. I think all this catering to strangers is rotting your brain, girl. Now move out of my way. I have better things to do than stand around watching you hide from life."

"I do not hide from life," Abby objected. "I have a

very full life and a busy one. And what could you possibly have to do with everyone's meal ready?"

"I have dinner to arrange. All your current guests have elected to upgrade and have dinner here this evening. I'm going Italian tonight. I want to get started on the fresh pasta."

Abby scowled. "Wait a minute. All? Even Colin and his daughter?"

"Yup. Even them. I think you'd better get used to him being around." Genevieve grinned.

Abby did just the opposite. "I thought he'd be leaving today. He knows I don't want him here and he didn't really want to stay here, either."

"Since when do you discourage a paying customer from staying? And why wouldn't he want to stay here? It's the nicest B and B in the area." Her focus sharpened more. "Why do I get the feeling there's a history here?"

"Colin McCarthy is poison. Let's just leave it at that."

Genevieve was one of the newer residents of the area. The only McCarthy family member she'd ever met was Erin. Colin's youngest sister had stayed at Cliff Walk when she'd revisited the area on her way home from college that spring. Abby prayed Genevieve didn't ask any more questions. Her anger at Colin was too personal and too deep to talk about. She never had and she never would.

She put her hand on the door and glanced at Genevieve. "The little girl's scrambled eggs are getting cold," she grumbled pointedly and pushed through the door. The cook had no choice but to follow since Abby stood holding the door open for her.

Abby should have been ready to face Colin. But then she heard his rich baritone voice telling Jessie her breakfast had arrived. Abby's legs started to quake as memories washed over her—that voice teasing her sweetly, whispering sexual praises in her ear one minute and rejecting her the next.

She turned away. "Enjoy your eggs, sweetheart," she managed to say, as Genevieve placed the plate in front of Jessie. Then, trying to stay as far away from Colin as possible, Abby walked across the room to stand closer to the door of her office. "Has everyone made plans for the day?" she asked, and nearly sighed in relief when an elderly guest, Mr. Kane, nodded.

"We hoped to go into town," he said. "Is the road clear yet?"

Abby shook her head. "I called the state police a short while ago. The rock slide should be cleared by around three this afternoon but not before. You can still go into town, though." She gave them alternate directions that would take them into New Jersey and to the town across the river from Hopetown. "The bridge there is open and you'll cross back into Pennsylvania right in the heart of Hopetown. Silly as it sounds, it's actually faster, though nowhere near as quaint or scenic. You may enjoy exploring their shops, too."

She stepped into her office then, pleased that she'd managed to keep her eyes off Colin. She picked up a pile of the brochures she'd put together with a map showing the alternate route into Hopetown and the written directions.

Unfortunately, Colin was speaking when she stepped back into the dining room and her eyes zinged right to him as if they had no will of their own. He glanced her way at the exact moment her gaze landed on him. He stopped mid-sentence for a long beat and they stared at each other. There was something turbulent in his eyes, then he blinked and looked away, finishing his comment to Mr. Kane.

Abby gave the elderly gentleman the stack of brochures to pass along the table to anyone who wanted one. She was thankful Mr. Kane was seated the farthest from Colin and so gave her all the excuse she needed to stay far away from her newest customer. Jessie was engrossed in her breakfast, but Colin looked up and their gazes locked once more—and held longer than they should have.

"You look pretty today, Miss Abby. Just like a princess," Jessie said, looking up from her eggs.

Abby dragged her attention off Colin, grateful for Jessie's comment. But it also surprised Abby, upon further examination, since all her clothes were essentially the same boring style. Her trendy oldest sister, Caroline, said Abby's long, flowing skirts and Victorian-style blouses were matronly. Caroline or anyone else could call them what they wanted but, however they looked, Abby felt safe in them. She could hide in the soft layers. She did not feel at all like a princess. She was supposed to be an ice queen so she'd never be tempted to risk her heart again.

"Yep, all she needs is a tiara," Colin quipped silkily. There were chuckles, and speculation suddenly twinkled in the eyes of most of the other guests. Abby refused to take Colin's remark as flirting the way they apparently had. It was more likely a taunt about her privileged upbringing.

Besides no one flirted with her. And that was the way she wanted it.

And even if for some perverse reason he had been flirting, it was Colin McCarthy—so it meant nothing. Nothing at all.

Abby forced herself to smile pleasantly. She wasn't going to let him ruin her calm existence or cause speculation and gossip about her.

"Thank you, Jessie. If you'll all excuse me, I have some housekeeping chores to take care of," Abby said. Then she turned to move toward her office again, holding her head high, retreating in as dignified a manner as she could manage.

Colin's mind reeled. She was going off to *what?* Make beds and dust? What had happened to the rich daddy's girl he'd once known?

He shook his head. He shouldn't care.

Colin looked back down at his half-eaten breakfast, too agitated to finish. All through his meal, helplessly unable to look away, he'd watched Abby as she'd chatted with her other guests. The conclusion he'd reached was that though he didn't want to be, he was still as attracted to Abby Hopewell as he'd been years ago. And that made him feel unsettled, uncomfortable and just plain stupid.

He gave up on breakfast and hustled Jessie out to the pickup. Once he had them both belted in, he pulled the bottle of antacids out of the glove box and ate a handful, damning Abby for causing the familiar pain in his belly to blossom once again.

Then he looked back up at the Victorian he hadn't yet seen in the light of day. It was perfect.

Every period detail was right on the money. Even the porch furniture was a trip back in time.

All of which meant Abby was probably the only woman he'd ever met who would understand his love for restoration and his obsession with historical accuracy.

At that moment Jessie squealed and bounced up and down in her seat. "Look at all the plants, Daddy. And what's those bunch of houses over there?"

"I noticed them last night, but I don't think they're houses. One of the people at breakfast said something about visiting the Hopewell's winery. And those plants are grape vines."

"There sure are lots of them and that wine-ry is real pretty. Not as special as Abby's Castle but it's pretty."

"It's call Cliff Walk, kitten, not Abby's Castle," Colin told his starry-eyed daughter.

"I still think it's her castle. She even lives in the tower just like Rapunzel. Maybe that's her town over there, Daddy," Jessie speculated, her mind hopping subjects again.

Colin looked back at the B and B and noticed Abby staring out a window at them—her expression frozen in sadness. "I want to find out what it's all about," he said, his mind occupied with questions other than Jessie's.

"They look a little like our old house but different, too," Jessie went on, sounding as confused as he felt.

He mentally shook himself. Their home had had Spanish influences, like so many others in Southern California. This was subtly different. In the light of day he saw it was definitely Tuscan.

"Actually I think this is Italian. It looks like a village I visited in Italy when I was in the army. That's where Mrs. Hopewell is from."

Jessie's smooth brow puckered with deep thought. "There's so many new peoples here. Who Mrs. Hopewell is, Daddy?"

Colin smiled. "That would be Abby's mom. Let's go exploring before we head over to the house." Maybe he'd get some questions answered from the queen mother.

"Am I still gonna have to stay in the living room and on the porch when we get to Torthúil?"

"It's no different than usual when I start on a house. Till I get the place inspected, and find out for sure where you're safe, you stay put in the rooms I've checked out."

"But we don't have the trailer no more. You said this time—"

"I was wrong, partner. Daddies can make mistakes." And wasn't that an understatement, considering who owned the house where they were staying and the mess the one he owned was in. "It's been years since I was here," he continued as they drew closer to the little Hopewell village that made him feel as if they'd stepped right into the pages of a tour book on Tuscany. "I guess I remembered Torthúil the way it was when I left."

She gave him a long-suffering sigh. "Then let's go 'sploring. It's better than not doin' nothin' at Torthúil. Why Gram didn't fix the roof when it got old?"

"No one's lived in it for years. A small farm like Gram's in Florida doesn't make enough money to survive down there *and* fix up a house she doesn't live in up here. Nobody who saw the house told me we needed a new roof or I'd have gotten it fixed. I wish they had but—"

"Look at that big doggie!" Jessie shrieked in his ear. "Isn't he won'erful?"

Big? He was massive. The Hopewells had a dog? A *big* dog? Things certainly had changed. "You sure it's a dog, kitten? Looks more like a horse to me."

Jessie giggled, strained to sit taller the closer he drove so she could still see the leaping canine monster. Colin parked in the crushed-granite parking lot labeled Visitor Parking, then unbuckled Jessie from her booster seat behind him. He swung her in front of him where she usually took the opportunity to grab the wheel to pretend driving. Today the dog took all her attention, leaping around like a goat as he chased a ball thrown by a tall blond boy who looked about nine or ten.

Colin decided that no matter how affectionate the dog seemed, he wasn't putting Jessie down to get trampled. But he needn't have worried about the animal jumping on her or knocking her down. Instead he galloped over and all but fell at Colin's feet, presenting his belly for scratching. The boy followed and obliged his pet.

"Can I pet him?" Jessie gazed at Colin with pleading eyes. At that moment he silently promised to get her the puppy she'd been asking for since she turned three.

"Sure you can pet him," the blond boy said. "You could probably use him for a pillow. I do all the time."

Carefully and slowly, Colin eased Jessie to the ground. All the big dog did was let his tongue loll out of his mouth and pant harder as Jessie none too gently moved her hand over his belly. Then he put his head back and moaned in ecstacy.

Jessie giggled. "He's funny."

"My dad calls him a character," the boy said. "My uncle Nic bought him for me the day they brought my new baby cousin home to Hopewell Manor from the hospital."

"Actually, if you remember, Uncle Nic bought him for your cousin," a woman said from behind them. "Lucky for you Thunder's a little too big for a premature newborn."

"I never thought I'd see the day dogs were allowed at Hopewell Manor," Colin remarked absently, waiting for Juliana Hopewell to recognize him.

She walked out the door of the nearby building and cocked her head, her eyes narrowed as if in thought. He was ready for another hard-as-emerald stare when she realized who he was, but instead her green eyes lit with delight. "Colin McCarthy? My Lord, but you remind me of Tracy. And actually Thunder only visits the manor. This is Jamie. He's Caroline's son. They live in a house they built toward the back of the winery property.

"The baby Thunder was originally bought for is Sammie's. Nikki was just barely five pounds the day she came home. Her father was rushing his fences a bit and overjoyed at finally getting her home." She chuckled. "So, besides having a lovely little girl of your own, how are you, Colin? And what are you doing back here after so many years?"

Apparently James Hopewell hadn't shared with his wife what had happened between Colin and Abby. Well, he wouldn't be rude to Juliana when she obviously hadn't had anything to do with what her husband had done. Besides, from what he'd heard, she'd been on the receiving end of Hopewell's cruelty herself.

"I came back to live at Torthúil, but the house is in much worse shape than I'd thought it would be. Jessie and I are staying at Cliff Walk until I can renovate it. We arrived in the middle of the storm last night. It was pretty dark so I didn't get to see everything you've done here." He made a sweeping gesture toward what he could now see was indeed a replica of a Tuscan town square surrounded by four buildings. They were laid out like four sides of a pentagon, leaving the square and the fifth side open to a view of the vines that terraced down the hillside toward the cliffs.

"The girls and I started all this after their father died. This building is the headquarters of Hopewell Winery." She pointed left. "That one is the winery itself. It houses the gift shop, tasting room and some of the machinery. We had the wine cellars blasted into the rock and they're below us. And this building and the one at the far end of the court is Bella Villa. It's a banquet facility. There are three halls between the two buildings and our offices."

"I hadn't heard about any of this. I was also surprised to find Abby at Cliff Walk last night."

"Oh," she said, sounding somewhat distressed. "I'd better make sure she's all right. You know, Tracy's death devastated her, even though they'd drifted apart that last summer. Seeing you probably brought it all up for her again. I imagine coming home for the first time since then did the same for you. That was terribly mean of your commander not to let you come home for your own sister's funeral." She reached out and took his hand. "I am so sorry for your losses. I know you and Tracy were close. And we heard about your father's death when Erin stayed here in May."

She frowned. "*Was* Abby very upset when she saw you again?"

"I suppose she was," Colin said carefully, his mind whirling once again. Abby and Tracy hadn't been close that summer? They'd practically been sisters for years. What could have happened between them? He wished now that he hadn't told his parents he never wanted to hear Abby's name again. And he wished they hadn't listened.

"She did take your sister's death so hard. After that, and my divorce from her father, Abby was never really the same." Juliana looked over toward Cliff Walk, then blinked, seeming to realize that perhaps she'd said too much. She cleared her throat as if to punctuate a change in subject. "So, how about the two-dollar tour? If we're going to be neighbors again, you should know what's going on up here on the plateau."

Juliana Hopewell had no idea how much Colin wanted to figure out exactly what was going on. And what had gone on in his absence. "I think I'll take you up on that.

"Jessie," he called, noticing the boy and his dog had led his daughter farther away than he was comfortable with. They were going toward the middle of the plateau, where all the Hopewell enterprises sat, and he remembered the cliffs that led down from there. He and his buddies had even climbed them in their daredevil teens. And Jessie tended to be more of a daredevil than he'd ever been at her age. No way did he want her finding out about those rocky cliffs.

When she arrived back at his side, Colin took her hand. "Mrs. Hopewell said she'd take us to see all the buildings."

Jessie frowned up at him. "Can't I stay and play with the doggie?"

"Jamie, you come, too," Juliana called to her grandson. "Thunder can be along for part of the tour," Juliana told the boy. Then she turned back to Colin and explained, "I'm designated sitter for the next two hours. Oh, by the way, if you're planning on a dog, I'd like to recommend the shelter in Hopetown."

"An animal shelter? Isn't that a little out of character for Hopetown? Last I remember, the good citizens would rather drown a mutt than house it till it was adopted."

Juliana Hopewell arched on elegant eyebrow. She was a beautiful woman even as she must be nearing her fifties. "Maybe the Hopetown of ten years ago, but a lot has changed around here in the last several years. You'll see." She turned away, gestured to the grapevines growing in terraced rows and started what he imagined was a routine tour. "We started with fifty-three thousand young plants cloned from the finest European stock. The family buried each plant in winter for..."

Colin, both children and the dog followed her inside the winery. And within minutes, Jessie was as enthralled as he was with the big kettles and presses and stack after stack of barrels in the cellar. He was pleasantly surprised by the few sips of the wines he tried. Hopewell produced a top-shelf product. He enjoyed the tour especially because James Hopewell was probably spinning in his grave. His ex-wife and daughters had lent his prestigious family name to several establishments he'd have considered beneath him.

Juliana was CEO of all three family-owned businesses. Caroline Hopewell Westerly was CFO of the winery and Bella Villa. Samantha was in charge of the farming and the winery operations, which really would have frosted her father. And Abby was entirely in charge of Cliff Walk and was also PR director for all the Hopewell enterprises.

After the tour, Colin spent the rest of the day at Torthùil, tearing out the destroyed plaster ceilings and walls and cataloguing the changes he planned to make. He did everything with an eye toward preserving the hundred-and-fifty-year tradition of the classic colonial farmhouse built by Liam McCarthy, an ancestor back in the 1860s for whom his father had been named.

But hard labor couldn't keep questions about Abby from his mind. He remembered the adventurous, happy girl he'd fished out of the river who'd become fast friends with his sister. She'd been impulsive and mischievous, yet generous and good-hearted. Then he'd come home for Christmas six months after joining the army to find a new Abby. She was still the coltish teen he'd left behind, but she was quieter and more reserved than he'd remembered. Then he'd gone home for Tracy's graduation and found Abby had turned into a siren who'd all but forced him to dance with her at the graduation party his parents had thrown for both girls. It was later that night that his barriers had fallen and he'd let her pull him in with her sensual innocence, trapping his mind and heart.

And then there was now. She was uptight, prissy and cold. But, that said, there was also a bit of the old Abby in the way she treated Jessie. It was probably just her good business sense, he told himself. As long as she catered to Jessie, the other guests would approve, preserving their good image of Cliff Walk and its proprietor.

He'd gone looking for answers and had only come up with more questions about the past—and more problems with the present. What had happened between Abby and Tracy? And if she and Abby had no longer been friends, then that meant Abby had had no part in his sister's death.

Colin didn't know where today's glimpse into those months between his departure and Tracy's death left him, but one thing was clear.

He needed answers.

And once he had them, Colin wasn't sure he'd like them.

Not one little bit.

Chapter Four

Abby spent the evening and all the next day trying to avoid Colin at every turn.

She was too busy to waste time worrying about the past and the particularly annoying customer in her present. That's all Colin was.

She had to focus—she was planning to attend a meeting at the town hall that night, and she was anxious to see Harley Bryant's reaction to her now that she was officially on the ballot to run against him in November's mayoral election.

As dinner approached, Abby changed into a light summer suit and pinned her hair up in the no-nonsense style appropriate for tonight's meeting of the zoning commission. As a candidate for the mayor of Hopetown, she needed to project a serious and businesslike image. She'd never have run for public office, but Harley Bryant had to be ousted before he ran Hopetown into the ground. More than once Harley had shamelessly used his position as mayor to further his own agenda, one that seemed to include destroying everything her mother and sisters had worked to build. She'd more or less been drafted by the chamber of commerce and other concerned citizens, and initially she'd felt she had no choice but to run for the office. But now she wanted to beat him. She wanted him contained and silenced so that his wheeling and dealing could only hurt those who chose to do business with Bryant Savings and Loan, his family business.

To get into town, Abby planned to borrow the little Mercedes she and her mother shared. Abby knew she had some time before Juliana arrived with the car. She'd dropped her mother off at the manor, then zip down the winding road into Hopetown. Anxious to be on her way, she settled into one of the big wicker rockers on the porch to wait.

It was only a routine meeting tonight and since she was well prepared, Abby let her mind wander as she stared out over the terraces of ripening vines. Before she knew it, her mind veered to thoughts of Colin. Then the porch squeaked behind her.

Startled by the intrusion, Abby turned. As if conjured by her thoughts, he stood just outside the front door. From the look of surprise on his handsome face, she was sure he was just as unprepared as she was to find themselves alone together.

"I didn't expect to see you here," he said.

"Why not? I told you I live here," she replied, recovering quickly despite her racing heart.

A smirk crossed his features. "That's what I hear, but you couldn't prove it by how scarce the Snow White sightings have been. Jessie's going to drive me crazy asking where you are. Are you hiding from us, *Miss* Abby?"

Abby stood, her lips clamped together to keep herself from answering truthfully that she was hiding from *him*. As she tried to walk away, he put a hand on her arm to stop her retreat. Her racing heart now thundered at his touch. Pointedly, Abby looked down at his hand, then defiantly back up at him.

Her gaze locked with his. He stared. She stared. Unable to look away, she nearly sighed in relief when a piping voice said joyously, "Miss Abby! You're here! Daddy found you."

Colin blinked and dropped his hand from her arm as if burned. "She's here. We were just talking about old times," he lied—but not very smoothly. His voice sounded rough, as though his throat was dry. He coughed a little then went on, "Abby wasn't so hard to find when I lived around here before. In fact, our family couldn't seem to get rid of her. She was always around because she was your Aunt Tracy's best friend."

"Aunt Tracy's the one who got dead, right?"

"Yes." He coughed again, clearly fighting emotion. "When she was eighteen," he amended. From the thin line of his lips and the angry flare in his eyes, Abby guessed he'd remembered not just Tracy's death but his inability to attend the funeral.

Well, she carried a lot of anger about Tracy's death too—but it was directed at Colin. If Tracy had still been her friend, she would have listened to the truth about Kiel Laughlin when Abby tried to tell her. Tracy had had one huge fault—money. Feeling the lack of it, and desperately wanting it. She'd seen Abby's mother's life as a fairy tale come true. And she'd thought Kiel was her Prince Charming.

But Kiel was spoiled and reckless. One day while Tracy stood on the bow of his father's boat, Kiel took his eyes off the river to take another swig of his beer. He ran them aground at high rate of speed and Tracy broke her neck when she flew off and landed in the shallow water. He'd been charged with manslaughter. There hadn't been any witnesses on the shore, though, and the one witness against him had changed her story at the last minute. Everyone else on the boat had always claimed to have been looking the other way. With no evidence, Kiel had been found not guilty.

Tracy had been with Kiel for one reason—to capture him and his wealth. She hadn't understood that the real treasure was a marriage like Tracy's parents had shared. No matter the lack of material goods, the McCarthys' marriage had been one made in heaven.

No so with the Hopewells. Abby's mother had found wealth when she wed her husband but within months of Tracy's death, the marriage dissolved.

It was only after ending her last attempt at a relationship that Abby had come to understand that she had to put the lessons of that painful summer to work in her own life. She would never again let a man get close to her. She was impulsive and had a passionate nature that would surely lead her to heartbreak again and again. Abby knew what a dangerous combination those could be just by looking at the mess her father had made of all their lives.

James Hopewell had gone on a tour of Europe after graduation from college. While in Tuscany he'd met Juliana and was swept away by passion for the seventeen-year-old daughter of a local vintner. He'd married her in spite of her father's objections, then he'd brought his young wife home, where he'd found his own parents no less displeased by the union.

Years later he'd once again impulsively succumbed to his craving for passion and he'd betrayed Juliana. It was only months after Abby's own debacle with Colin, and Tracy's death, that her mother discovered James in the arms of another woman. Then her oldest sister's heart had been broken when her fiancé called off their engagement because of the scandal surrounding the family.

Lesson learned.

That was why Abby had spent these past years studiously hiding behind a carefully built wall of self-discipline and self-denial. She couldn't trust her own judgment. Not where men—and certainly not love—were concerned.

And she never would.

"...so after that," Abby heard Colin saying, seemingly from a distance, "when you saw my sister, Tracy, you nearly always saw Abby Hopewell."

Abby winced as memories and emotions flooded her thoughts. The pain of Tracy's death had never really dulled as Abby had been promised it would. Much as she blamed Colin for somehow causing the rift between them, she blamed herself just as much for giving Tracy a craving for the kinds of things only money could buy.

Abby shook off the painful memories. "If you'll excuse me, I have to meet my mother," she lied, and fled down the porch steps. She'd wait for Juliana over at the winery even if she broke her neck stomping along the cracked-stone driveway in her high heels.

As she entered the town hall at exactly two minutes to seven, Abby looked around for her core group of lovable troublemakers. Sure enough, they were all there, seated down front and ready for action. Jean Anne, co-owner of the Hopetown Hotel and the Blue Moon Restaurant and Bar, turned around and waved to the seat they'd saved her. Jerry, Jean Anne's husband, wasn't there—probably the one home minding the kids and the hotel. As Abby strode down the center aisle, Harry Clark, owner of a local biker boutique, stood and turned toward her. Deep frown lines wrinkled his forehead. Harry looked like the kind of man you wouldn't want to meet in a dark alley—or even mess with in broad daylight—but he was a pussycat.

"What's up?" she asked, seeing that even Muriel Haversham seemed disturbed.

Muriel was the owner of Seek and Find, one of the many antique stores that dotted the town. She was usually unflappable and sunny. She didn't look a bit sunny tonight. "Harley's changed the agenda—tabled the federal grant discussion."

Abby frowned. "What could be more important than getting federal help to solve the town's flooding problem? Is he waiting for a fourth flood? Three in the last eighteen months isn't enough?"

Harry waved the agenda. She stooped down and picked a copy off the chair she was apparently meant to occupy. "It just says development."

"I don't like the mystery," Harry grumbled. "He's probably trying to use tonight as a platform for his reelection. He'll probably start trying to blame the Hopewell complex for the flooding again."

"Don't worry," she promised. "I'm not about to let Harley Bryant get away with any posturing or diversionary tactics. When they did the perk test to check for our drainage it proved nothing runs off that plateau."

"We have confidence in you, kid," Albert Canter

said in his gruff voice. Al was a blacksmith and seventy-five if he was a day. For any tourist who asked, he demonstrated his craft as gleefully as he displayed and sold his handcrafted iron work. Al just loved the town he'd retired to. He still considered himself retired even though he probably worked sixty-hour weeks during tourist season. Which had pretty much become year-round for the town.

After she took her seat, a steady stream of interested citizens entered the hall. Abby wished some of the other business owners would stand up to Harley, but she'd come to understand that going against him was uncomfortable for them. Some had spouses or children who worked for Harley at Bryant Savings and Loan. Others were friendly with Shirley Bryant—the shy, lovely woman he'd won over to the shock of nearly everyone in town. Still others had known his parents. Hopetown remained a small town, despite the large tourist trade.

Before long, Harley sauntered toward the podium and tapped on the microphone. "Can I have your attention?"

Just then the doors at the back of the hall opened and drew all eyes, Abby's included. Colin McCarthy walked boldly up to the front row on the left side of the small hall. He turned toward Abby and grinned before sitting down. He certainly seemed to be jumping into life in Hopetown quickly, she thought cynically.

Abby straightened her shoulders, refusing to let him

see that his mere presence set her on edge. Then Harley began speaking. "I'm sure you're all wondering why I tabled the grant discussion tonight. First off, we have six months after our little water problem along Main to deal with that application. Second, I don't have figures from everyone, so if that includes you, get them to my office. And third, I have something more exciting to talk about tonight. I'd like to introduce my old friend, Colin McCarthy. Colin, come on up and get re-acquainted with everyone."

Colin stood and loped confidently up to the podium as Bryant continued, "Colin has returned to Hopetown as quite a success story. An award-winning architect and successful builder on the Left Coast, he's come back here to live and to make Hopetown part of his next venture. I'm asking the zoning board for rezoning and an acreage variance on the land Colin owns so we can expedite matters and get the ball moving on his project. This will be a real shot in the arm for the town's coffers. Colin, suppose you give us a brief explanation of your plans."

"Thanks, Harley," Colin said, looking unruffled and self-assured as he stepped to the microphone in spite of grumbling from some in the audience. "I've returned to develop the land that was the site of my family's farm for generations."

Abby couldn't believe what she was hearing. Develop upstream from the town? Was Colin off his rocker? Was Harley?

"Torthúil Gardens will be a townhouse and condo

community with a large segment along the river dedicated to over fifty-five adult living surrounded by condo-association-owned land," Colin went on. "In this way we limit population increases of school-age children and the burden of increasing property taxes to fund new schools. I'm also considering a clubhouse, pool and exercise center that any resident of Hopetown can use with the purchase of an annual membership."

The grumbling grew louder as Colin put up his hand, quieting everyone. "This is all in the proposal stages. I should be ready with detailed drawings and plans within a few weeks."

Then Harley spoke. "I'm proud to have secured the financing Colin needs for this project. The tax revenue alone will do more for Hopetown than any federal grant."

Abby popped up out of her seat. "And if you develop Torthúil the way it sounds like you plan to, you'll need even bigger federal grants to clean up the mess the additional run-off will cause the town." Shouts of agreement came from pockets around the room.

"Harley, how can you even consider this after all the flooding?" she demanded. "Oh, wait," she continued, narrowing her eyes as she stared Bryant down. "Since you secured the financing, your bank'll make a bundle on this, won't it? But what's the tax base going to look like if there's no town left, Harley?"

She turned toward the zoning board. Her family had tangled with most of them before. "I beg all of you to remember that this town is about more than tax revenue. It's our duty as Hopetown citizens to guard our historical landmarks. I urge the committee to table this discussion for tonight and consider carefully any plans submitted.

"And I'd like to remind you all how hard Harley Bryant fought behind the scenes to keep my family from expanding our operation." She knew he'd wanted them to fail so his bank would be free to foreclose and gain control of the winery. Unfortunately she had no proof. "I'd also like to remind you that because we sit so high, we have hundreds more feet of drainage under our complex than Torthúil. Plus, a very large percentage of the plateau where our facility sits was always planned as farmland and a nature preserve. The perk tests you all reviewed proved our use of the land has zero impact on the river."

Abby finally took a chance and looked up at Colin. His jaw was rock hard, his eyes cold as he stared down at her. She glanced away and over to where the zoning board sat.

After a few moments' deliberation, they approved only the proposed work on Colin's farmhouse, tabling further discussion until the August meeting when his plans were called on to be ready for consideration. Colin had lost this round. And would lose the next, and the next, and the next if she had anything to say about it.

She'd fight the devil himself to save the town named for and founded by her ancestor Josiah Hopewell.

Hopetown had been on the banks of the Delaware River since 1689, and no money-grubbing builder was going to help wipe it off the map.

Hopetown had been hit by three major floods in the past eighteen months, the runoff that endangered many homes and roads was caused by too much development in the entire watershed region. Colin's plans would only increase the runoff just upstream, dangerously close to town.

The Hopewell name still meant something around there and she'd use every bit of influence it gave her. She'd beat Colin McCarthy and see his dreams crushed.

Just the way he'd crushed hers.

Chapter Five

Colin stood in the shadow of one of the big oaks that shaded the oldest section of Main Street, waiting for Abby to leave the meeting. He'd spent the past ten minutes trying once again to control his temper, which seemed to flare where she was concerned.

Earlier in the evening, when he'd run into her on the porch, he'd purposely brought up Tracy to see her reaction. Juliana Hopewell was right. Abby still deeply mourned his little sister.

Knowing that, he had to try to understand the past, so he'd called his mother. She'd confessed that his father had ordered Tracy to end her friendship with Abby. He'd told Tracy only that James Hopewell had threatened to ruin them financially if Abby had any contact with the McCarthys. He hadn't told Tracy the whole truth because they'd decided that in the short term they wouldn't tell any of the younger children what had happened. It had seemed unnecessary to risk upsetting them about the threat to their parents' livelihood.

Now, though, Colin needed to understand what had happened. Now he knew why Tracy and Abby had ended their friendship. Abby hadn't had a thing to do with Tracy's death. Which left him with no reason to be angry—and a boatload of leftover hunger for her that he could do nothing about.

Because, in spite of any attraction she still felt for him, she had every reason to think he'd used her that night. And for some reason she seemed to hold *him* responsible for what had happened to Tracy, which made no sense at all. It had been Abby, young and upset though she had been, who'd caved in to her father's demands and given away their secret.

Now she'd tried to torpedo his project, causing his anger to blaze anew. Once again the great and glorious Hopewell name alone was more important within the town than anything or anyone else.

Harley had made it plain that they needed this development to widen the town's tax base. And the McCarthy family needed it too. Torthúil had begun failing about a year before Tracy's death and that expense had nearly put them over the edge. It had been Liam McCarthy's dream to preserve the farm for future generations—to sell Torthúil would have broken his father's already wounded heart. But his daughter's death had left him a nearly broken man. They'd sold off all the expensive farm machinery to pay off the banknote and moved to Florida to improve their health—and forget the past.

After his father's death, Colin had gambled his and Jessie's future to parlay Torthúil's now worthless farmland into a tidy fortune. He'd sold everything, including his successful business, and moved home to live in the old house. He intended to keep several acres surrounding the house as a way of honoring his father's wishes while developing the rest of the property. It was the only practical solution he'd been able to think of. He'd designed and built award-winning projects of the same type in California, and he knew he could make Torthùil Gardens just as successful, for himself and the community.

He watched Abby from the shadows as she broke away from a cluster of people and walked to her car. In the fading evening light, Colin saw her smile fade when she noticed Harley watching her.

"If it isn't the ice maiden," the mayor sneered from across the street.

Abby crossed her arms. "What do you want, Harley?"

"You think you can get elected by wrecking the local economy?" Harley said as he approached her. "More people in that room are on our side than yours."

"Those people aren't the business owners who have kept this town alive and flourishing. They're the ones who go off to work somewhere else every day. Main Street *is* this town and it needs protecting. And so do the homes along River Road."

"And one of them is the precious Hopewell Manor. I'm not the only one being self-serving. I'll bury you in that election one way or another. You hear me?" he growled. Harley grabbed her arm and Colin saw her wince. "You don't know how to fight dirty. But I do."

Enough of watching from the shadows. Pushing away from the tree, Colin started forward. As he walked quietly toward them Abby tried to pull away from Harley but he hung on.

"Hey, Harley. How's it going?" Colin called out. As soon as Harley heard his voice, he dropped Abby's arm and turned his back on her nonchalantly, as if he hadn't just manhandled her. Harley hadn't changed. He was still a coward. Colin saw Abby subtly rub her arm and knew he'd been right to step in. Harley was the picture of innocence, though, with a cocky smile plastered on his face—a smile that made Colin wonder why he'd never noticed before how much Harley resembled a snake.

"You okay, Abby?" Colin asked. She nodded and he could see her fighting spirit recovering a little more as each second ticked by.

"I was just…uh…trying to talk sense into your opposition," Harley explained.

"Is that what it's called?" Colin wondered aloud. "I can fight my own battles, Harley. I always could."

"Look, don't you worry. This isn't going to be a

battle. Her opposition isn't going to matter. She and her family are no better than the rest of us."

"I never said we were," Abby said. "But we do represent something in Hopetown that you clearly don't understand."

"Oh, I understand. Just like I understand what's going on in your head right now. I know why you're out to get Colin."

"I am *not* out to get Colin. I'm out to protect the town."

"Don't give me that load of bull." Harley waved his hand, dismissing her. "You seduced him, but it didn't tie him to you like you thought it would. Instead, he used you, sent you off to bed and left town the next day. And you've been pissed about it for years."

Abby blinked, her eyes went wide and her jaw dropped open for just a second. Then she turned furious eyes on Colin.

But no one was more shocked by Harley's words than Colin. He didn't know if Abby had time to realize that, though, because Harley was on a roll and scarcely paused for breath.

"And your sisters are no better. You think everyone in town doesn't know Caroline and Samantha married into money to bail that winery out of trouble? Let's see, sex for money. That would mean they prostituted themselves to save your mother's crazy dream. You think that's what it sounds like, Colin, old buddy?"

What Colin thought was that he really didn't want his name and "buddy" coming out of Harley Bryant's mouth in the same sentence. "I think you've said enough, Harley."

Abby didn't seem to hear him. He watched in admiration as she gathered her dignity around her like a protective shield. She fisted shaking hands at her sides and came back at Harley. "My sisters married their husbands because they love them, you dirty-minded moron. And their husbands wouldn't have felt the need to invest in the winery if you hadn't been up to no good. For years you've been trying to steal everything we've worked so hard to build. You loaned Mama the money to expand, knowing our exact business plan. Then you pulled strings on the zoning board to cause the building delays that nearly put us under. *That's* what the whole town knows, Harley. And if they don't, I'll make sure they find out," she finished, her voice icy but full of righteous anger. Then she spun away and got into the car.

Colin noticed several people had turned toward them. He hoped no one had gotten close enough to hear Harley's snide reference to the night between him and Abby.

That Harley spoke about the incident with such certainty surprised Colin. Harley hadn't said a word on the subject after Colin denied sleeping with Abby and she'd fled the kitchen in tears. So Colin had assumed his diversion had worked. That he hadn't hurt Abby for nothing.

Harley turned away now and headed back toward the other side of the street as Abby pulled away from the curb. The hatred he'd shown toward her worried Colin.

He caught up with Harley, thinking about the past as they walked silently through town. Nothing seemed to be what Colin had believed it to be. Abby confessing to her father had never made less sense. He'd had five sisters. Any one of them would have done anything to avoid telling their father that they'd just lost their virginity. It especially didn't fit with a girl who'd idolized her father the way Abby had. Why had he never thought of that? He shook his head, admitting the truth. Because he'd been so angry at her, and being angry had made never seeing her again so much easier.

Could it be that James Hopewell had not found out about their midnight encounter from Abby but from someone else? Suspicious, Colin looked at Harley. He'd been fun back when they were in high school, always ready for a laugh or some minor mischief, but his charm had begun to wear thin by that last time Colin was home. He'd thought his military experience had matured him faster than Harley's college experience had him.

Now that he'd seen the way he'd treated Abby, Colin realized he'd been well on the way to not liking the man Harley had become. He'd sensed even then that he couldn't trust him, and obviously the man had gotten worse with age instead of better.

Harley stopped and squeezed the back of his neck as he looked up the steps of the hotel. He stared at the door leading to the Blue Moon Bar, nestled into a corner of the building. "I could really use something to drink. What do you say we go help hold up the bar for a few hours?" He sighed. "I don't know why I let that snippy broad get to me the way I do. I'm smarter than she is. And come November, I'm going to rub her nose in it."

Colin followed, still trying to think about how Harley could have figured into that visit from James Hopewell. After an hour at the Blue Moon, Jerry Mooney, the hotel's owner, came in to relieve the bartender. He and Colin chatted, reminiscing about old times for a few minutes. During their short exchange, Jerry's displeasure with Harley became obvious, as well as his worry over the development plans and the flood problems Abby had mentioned.

When Harley started to get a little sloppy and loud, Jerry steered arriving customers toward the booths and stools up at the other end of the long narrow room. He'd joked that it was his way of keeping the tourists from being bothered by the town's drunken mayor.

Colin meanwhile continued to nurse his second beer, wondering if he'd ever find a way to get Harley to admit what he'd done. As Harley drank one bourbon on the rocks after another and began to slur his speech and brag, Colin tried steering the conversation toward Abby and the past. But every time Colin got near the subject of that night, Harley would pull back and veer off in another direction.

Colin grew more and more frustrated with the situation. He was stuck there with Harley when he had to get home to Jess—Cliff Walk's chef had jumped at the chance to babysit. Yet he wanted to get some answers. After a quick cell call to check on Jessie, who'd apparently fallen into a sound sleep and was content, Colin decided on the direct approach. He looked down the bar and noticed that he and Harley were now alone, except for some French-speaking tourists in a corner booth. Convinced he wouldn't be overheard, Colin finally said as casually as he could, "So you figured out that I'd been with Abby that night."

"For all the good it did me," Harley scoffed.

Okay, now that was a weird leap. "What did you expect my relationship with Abby to do for you?" he asked, trying for a lighthearted tone and failing miserably, suspicion creeping into his tone.

In the mirror Colin saw near rage reflected in Harley's eyes and realized more had happened than he'd suspected. But he still wasn't ready for the full scope of the truth.

"I went to old man Hopewell, you dope. Told him his angel child had been a bad little girl the night before."

"Why would you do that! What did Abby ever do to you?"

"Nothing. But I wanted things I knew Hopewell had power to get me so I went after them the only way I could. My father told me Hopewell had friends in high places. So I told Hopewell I'd give him the name of the guy she'd been with if he got me into an investment firm in the Big Apple." Harley shrugged carelessly. "He promised, so I gave you up."

Colin narrowed his eyes. "Were we ever friends?"

Harley snorted. "Were we? I don't know. I seem to remember you trying out for the football team and getting the quarterback spot I'd had all sewn up. Would a friend do that?"

"For God's sake, Harley. That was high school!"

"What harm did me telling him really do, anyway? You had your own thing going with the army and when that was over you were already signed up for UCLA in the fall. There was nothing he could do to you. You were already free of this place. I mean, it wasn't like she was still jailbait. Nothing happened to you."

Clenching his fist under the cover of the bar, Colin dropped any pretense of friendship. He kept his voice quiet. Deadly quiet. "Because of you I never got the chance to apologize to Abby for the things I said that night."

Harley blinked drunkenly. "Then why the hell'd you say them? I thought you didn't care about her."

"I was trying to protect her from your big mouth." He glared at Harley. "Hopewell came calling before I had a chance to see her the next day. He ordered me out of town and threatened my parents. He had your father's promise to foreclose on the farm if I refused. If Abby had turned up pregnant, nothing would have saved Torthúil. When Tracy died, he threatened the farm again if I came home for my little sister's funeral. And you destroyed any chance I might have had with Abby."

"Oh, please. You got married and had a kid so you

sure as hell haven't spent the last nine years pining for her. And Hopewell didn't honor the deal anyway. I knew he went to my father, because he threatened the bank, too. Said if I told anyone else, he'd pull his accounts out of the bank and take his partner and as many friends as he could with him. I had plans to make it big, but I'm still right here answering to my father, thanks to the Hopewells. I may be president of the bank, but he's chairman of the board."

"Why the hell couldn't you have applied to investment firms in Philly or New York on your own?"

"Didn't have the grades," Harley groused as if he hadn't earned his poor average all on his own.

"You always took the easy way out." Colin stood. He really needed to get out of there. He needed to get home to Jessie and he needed to get away from Harley. "God, I can't believe I ever called you a friend. I'll start looking for new financing in the morning."

"Yeah? If you do, don't expect my help getting this thing through zoning. I'm the big fish in this small pond and you'd better not forget it. Oh, by the way, I actually told Hopewell I was trying to protect Abby because you'd only slept with her so you could brag."

Colin turned his back on Harley and stalked toward the exit. Another second and he'd have put the man through the wall. A drunken voice muttered something behind him but Colin ignored it. He had to. He didn't want to waste any more time worrying about a worm like Mayor Harley Bryant. There was too much history running through Colin's mind that needed rewriting.

And his first order of business after checking on Jessie would be to apologize to Abby for the way he'd treated her. He didn't know if he should even explain why he'd done it. That didn't seem to matter anymore. What did matter was that he find some way to make things right.

The only problem was, he didn't have any idea how to do that.

Chapter Six

Abby reclined in the deep wooden swing on Cliff Walk's wraparound porch, shutting out everything but the summer serenade of the tree frogs and crickets. With one foot on the railing she could give the swing a lazy push every once in a while. She needed to decompress after her upsetting evening—if she didn't get the meeting off her mind she'd never get a good night's sleep. And she needed one, because tomorrow would be a busy day.

Two couples planned to leave in the morning and three other guests were scheduled to arrive. That meant she had several rooms to turn around. And she'd have to move Colin and Jessie because an older couple who often came back to Cliff Walk had specifically reserved

Number Ten. Which meant she wouldn't be able to avoid seeing Colin.

But the thought of where she planned to move him and his adorable daughter put a smile on her face. She remembered Jessie's insistence early on that Abby was Snow White and that staying at Cliff Walk would make Jessie a princess, too. The room switch gave Abby the chance to make a small piece of Jessie's dream come true. She planned to put the little girl in the second-floor turret room. There was no better way to make Jessie feel like a princess. The room was decorated in varying shades of sky-blue but its centerpiece was a gilt crown-shaped cornice over the bed with sky-blue silk draperies flowing from it, framing the headboard. Matching drapes hung at the two windows and puddled gracefully on the floor.

The turret room connected through a neat little bath to a small TV/sitting room with a Murphy bed where Colin could sleep. This way he wouldn't need to go to bed when Jessie did.

All of a sudden, Colin appeared before her for the second time that night. She'd seen him through her window arriving hours after the meeting. She'd thought she was safe from him, but there he stood.

Abby wasn't ready for another battle but could see little else happening after finding out he'd told Harley about their long-ago encounter.

"I need to talk to you," Colin said, standing just at the corner of the house, highlighted by the carriage lights that bracketed the front door.

Abby decided to act as if tonight hadn't been a revelation. "You won't convince me to back down. You have no idea what your stupid development will do to Hopetown."

He shook his head. "Not about that. Please, this is important." He glanced upward then back down. "I left the window in our room open so I'd hear Jess if she woke up. We have to talk." He took a deep breath. "Abby, I swear I never told Harley what happened between us."

The sincerity in Colin's voice disarmed her. She looked away and set the swing moving again, trying to appear unruffled, as if the past was of no consequence—except it was anything but. Abby mentally cringed at the idea of the Hopewell name once again being linked to a scandal, even one as trivial as a teenage indiscretion that had happened a decade earlier. Her father's infidelity and his much publicized and foolhardy death had been enough, thank you very much. She'd spent years doing all kinds of volunteer work and being as circumspect as possible trying to repair the Hopewell name in their community. Now she was running for mayor in the hope of saving the town itself.

Knowing her face was completely in shadow gave her the confidence to tell a blatant lie. Abby pitched her voice low, mindful of Jessie's open window. "Whether you did or didn't is immaterial. He knows. And he'll hold it over my head if I rock the boat on this project of yours no matter who stands to get hurt."

"I didn't come home to hurt anyone. Especially not you," he said as he sank down on the railing and leaned against the porch column at his back.

"Now you care about my feelings? Please. I think I preferred you brutally honest." In the glow of the carriage lights, Abby saw several emotions cross his face. Anger. Regret. And resignation. His shoulders slumped a bit.

"I didn't think I was going to tell you everything, because I don't deserve a break after the way I treated you. Now I see that maybe you need to know.

"I *didn't* tell Harley. But he must have guessed the truth, which means I didn't throw him off the track at all. That makes the things I said to you so much worse because I hurt you for no reason."

As much as Abby had longed for an explanation, she really didn't want to hear this. Not now. Not so many years later. "Don't flatter yourself" was the best rejoinder she could come up with. But it did no good. He was obviously unwilling to leave her even a shred of pride.

"I saw how badly I hurt you and I've felt guilty about it for years."

"Well, don't. Lesson learned. I lived." She endured a stare that seemed determined to see into her heart. She wanted to squirm under his penetrating gaze but held herself rigid.

"I wish I could believe that," he said so quietly it was almost as if he'd been talking aloud to himself. "What you need to understand is that I wasn't denying what happened between us, Abby. Or how much you'd always meant to me. But I was rattled. I'd lost control of every secret desire I'd had since you turned fourteen. And even at eighteen you were so young and sheltered compared to me. I had years of school ahead of me. You did, too. I'd only just realized that I hadn't protected you. That could have blown both our futures all to hell and gone. Then, in the next breath, I had Harley to deal with, too."

Abby could hardly take in all he'd said. Secret desire for her? She shook off her need to recount words she'd once have given anything to hear. And now when it was too late.... "Why didn't you tell me all that the next morning? I was there till after nine. And if you were so worried about the lack of protection, why didn't you at least try to find out later if I was or wasn't pregnant?"

"Dear God, you weren't, were you?" he asked, his expression one of sheer horror. But then he shook his head. "No, of course you weren't. Torthúil would be long gone if you had been."

"Torthúil? What would your parents' farm have to do with me—with us?"

"More than you can imagine." Colin closed his eyes and took a deep breath. "All this is why I was out so late tonight. I had a drink with Harley tonight—I wanted to try and figure out everything that happened. Abby...he admitted that he told your father about us."

Abby sucked in a strangled breath. "What? Why would he *do* that?"

"He did it to garner your father's favor, hoping for a free ticket to a job in New York with your father's connections."

"But Harley was your friend."

Colin laughed bitterly. "Apparently not. All Harley cares about Harley. If it makes you feel any better, your father didn't honor his agreement and Harley's pissed as hell to still be here in Hopetown."

"Maybe that's why he's been such a thorn in our side." She shook her head. "I wish I could understand why Daddy never said a word about any of this to me," she managed, her mind spinning.

"Considering how nice your mother was to me yesterday, I don't think he said anything to her, either. But he had plenty to say to me and my parents the next morning. He told me to get out of town and stay out. I wasn't to see you again or make any contact with you. If I did he'd make sure my folks lost Torthúil. Same if you were pregnant. So since he left my parents alone, I figured there wasn't a baby."

The soothing sounds of the night had completely disappeared. Abby forced herself into a sitting position and put her feet on the porch floor, relieved that at least that seemed to be where she thought it should be. But the rest of the world felt beyond her reach.

All the years of doubting herself. Her judgment. Her feelings. It was her father's fault.

And Tracy.

Her father was the reason her friendship with Tracy ended. And the fallout just got worse. "Even Tracy's funeral? It wasn't your commander. My father wouldn't even let you come home for that, would he?" She didn't wait for an answer. She'd already learned all the things her father had been capable of doing. "I'm so sorry. No wonder you came back here hating me."

Colin shook his head, looking sad and regretful. "No. I never hated you. I was angry, yes. Mixed with a fair share of my own guilt." He looked down at the porch floor then back up. "He said you'd admitted to what happened between us. By doing that, you'd have endangered my parents and Torthúil."

Abby stared at him. "I'd never have told my father. He was always telling me my impulsiveness would get me in trouble and damage the family name."

"That's pretty ironic considering what your father did to your mother. Earlier tonight, after Harley said what he did to you, I realized that you'd never have told James. Which made me suspicious of Harley and how your father must have found out." He huffed out a deep breath. "There's one other thing I need to apologize for. Until your mother said something in passing about Tracy and that you weren't friends anymore that last summer, I blamed you for her death. You were always together, so I assumed she met Kiel Laughlin through you. I also assumed you'd have been part of the crowd on the boat that day."

Abby shook her head. Grief for all the destruction her actions that night had caused everyone weighed her down. Her eyes filled with tears. "Before you beat yourself up too much, I've blamed you for Tracy's death, too. I thought your parents wouldn't let us hang out together because you told them I was a bad influence or maybe they overheard you talking to Harley. I tried to warn Tracy that Kiel Laughlin was trouble, but she wouldn't listen. I thought if we'd still been close, she might have. I don't know how to tell you how sorry I am." Though she tried to fight back a sob, her tears overflowed. "Me...my father...what he threatened... Tracy's death was all my fault."

Colin shook his head, denial of her guilt screaming through him as her tears tore at his soul. He'd so horribly misjudged her. And he'd never been more ashamed. Tracy had been dead nearly nine years and Abby had never really recovered from her death. He felt compelled to go to her, comfort her.

It was the most natural thing to sit next to her and wrap his arm around her shoulders. Her scent enveloped him, a balm to his battered spirit. Somehow he needed to offer her at least that in return.

"We all share the blame, Ab. Your father was trying to protect you. Mine was trying to protect the land and his family. They both went too far. Mom says Dad told Tracy your father had threatened to ruin us if you remained connected to our family. To Tracy, keeping her living in what she saw as poverty would have been the ultimate threat. But she loved you or she wouldn't have been so angry."

He smiled, feeling sad and wistful remembering

his little sister and the convoluted way her mind had worked. "Actually if she'd known the truth, and if my parents' farm hadn't been on the line, she'd have moved heaven and earth to make sure we had a chance with each other."

Abby shrugged and her fine-boned shoulders moved under his arm, making him acutely aware of how delicate she was. "But my father wouldn't have had anything to threaten you with if I hadn't come on to you that night. All I thought about was what I wanted and that it might be my only chance to find you alone. You tried to discourage me."

"For about two-point-two seconds. I was older. More experienced. I should have just sent you back to my sister's room where you were supposed to be."

"There's one other thing I did," she said so quietly he had to lean forward to hear her. "I used to buy Tracy clothes and pass them off to your mother as my hand-me-downs. Tracy always joked about needing to find a rich husband to keep her in the style I'd gotten her accustomed to. I never realized she meant it till she went after Kiel and wouldn't let go."

"And that's the part of it that was Tracy's fault."

Abby sucked in a quick breath and slid sideways from under his arm. She turned in the swing to face him, her eyes wide in shock. "Tracy? How can you say it was her fault? She was the innocent victim."

Colin was through casting blame where it didn't belong. His understanding of all that had gone wrong that summer had been crystal clear since following

Harley into the Blue Moon. “No, she wasn’t an innocent victim. All you did was love my sister and give her things to make her happy. It sounds as if you saw her making a mistake and tried to tell her. She shut you out, didn’t she? I loved her, too, but she wasn’t any more perfect than the rest of us. The difference is her flaw turned out to be fatal.”

Abby seemed to consider that and then a tear rolled from the corner of her eye. “I still miss her,” she admitted. “I’m so sorry, Colin. So much went wrong and I still can’t help thinking I started the chain of events.”

Her sadness tore at Colin. Wanting to offer comfort, he drew her back into his arms. But this time her scent changed his intentions, turned up his growing hunger for her.

The feel of her body against his brought back that other time when she’d lain nestled in his arms in his bed. His fingertips sought the softness of her arm. He traced upward to her shoulder, then her chin. He tipped her face upward and gently kissed her lips.

But even though, this time comfort had been his first aim, his lips—his arms, his body—seemed to have their own agenda. Just like back then.

His arms gathered her close.

His lips deepened the kiss.

His body ignited.

He’d forgotten it could be like this. The overpowering need that could stop his heart one second and have it thundering the next.

He wanted—no, he needed—to fill himself with the essence of her. Sweet mint and lavender. Abby was everything that was soft, sweet woman, yet there was an unexpected sensuality hidden beneath her ladylike facade. He raked his hand through her thick, silky tresses and slanted his mouth more firmly over hers. In her arms, Colin felt as if he'd finally come home.

He let the hand holding her chin drift down the slim column of her neck. Her heart, too, thundered at the same galloping pace as his. Then he cupped her small firm breast and was gratified when her nipple pebbled beneath his touch.

She groaned in the back of her throat and tunneled her fingers in his hair, but then her breath hitched and everything changed in a heartbeat. Colin felt as if someone had dumped ice water on him when she stiffened. He broke the kiss and let her skitter away as she obviously wanted. So many emotions surged through him as he stared into her tortured eyes.

Mainly he felt bereft of her trust, once freely given and now apparently lost to the mistakes of the past. "Abby, I'm sorry. I started out trying to comfort you but you and I—"

"No," she interrupted. "It was my fault. I shouldn't have let myself..." She shook her head almost violently. "I don't do this sort of thing. I can't. This can't be trusted." She stood and backed away. "*I* can't be trusted," she added, then fled as if being chased by demons.

She probably was.

And they were demons he'd helped create.

Nothing was clearer to Colin in that moment than the effect the past had on Abby. It had overshadowed the woman she might have become. The nightmare of that summer had affected her mind and heart so much more than it had his. And he'd lived years believing he'd been the real victim.

He'd been so wrong.

His life had changed because he'd been made to feel inferior, but he'd used his anger to achieve his dreams. He'd come back to town bent on showing everyone how successful he'd become, knowing that was the best revenge he could have on the long-dead James Hopewell.

And now he was back where he needed to be, but the anger was gone. The drive to succeed was still there, along with his need to fulfill the promise of success he'd made to himself, but he realized that now his emotional focus had shifted to Abby.

It was hard to remember a time while growing up that Abby hadn't been important to him. Looking back, it became clear that Abby had always owned a piece of his heart. First as a sort of surrogate sister, even though he'd had five of his own. Then the summer he graduated from high school and Abby turned fourteen, that began to change. She'd come over to swim in the river just as she always had the first day of summer vacation.

He'd been in the water already coaxing his youngest sister, Erin, to jump into his arms. Abby had walked up behind her, trying to bolster little Erin's courage, and Colin had been struck dumb the moment his focus landed on Abby. Wearing a bikini with her thick black hair flowing loose about her shoulders, the fact that she was blossoming into a breathtaking woman had been as impossible to ignore as the effect she had on his unruly eighteen-year-old body. Horrified, he'd turned and dived for the deeper water of the river before his brain managed to clear enough to remember Erin.

Nothing had ever been the same between him and Abby again. It was one of the reasons he chose to go into the army instead of attending community college. He'd needed to get away from the temptation Abby presented. It hadn't worked because the minute she'd come on to him his barriers had fallen at practically the speed of light.

Tonight, her ultimate reaction to his kisses proved that something deep inside Abby had changed again. She'd lost her trust in him, which didn't surprise him, considering all that had happened. He'd need to earn it back, to try and rebuild that old friendship. But now that he was back for good, he didn't think he could be just friends with Abby. But he refused to be an enemy.

He wanted her.

As friend *and* lover.

With Jessie already so crazy for her, that left only one relationship that would work for him. Marriage. If there was one thing Colin was not, it was indecisive. He made up his mind about all manner of things quickly. Then he stuck by those decisions and made them work.

Sudden, maybe, but not unreasonable. The shared history was there. And there was the almost unreasonable attraction he'd felt for her since the day pigtails had given way to a flowing mane of hair. And she'd apparently always felt the same for him.

It was more than a plus that she was nuts about his kid. Jessie was innocent and it was his job to protect her. The only thing that would have given him pause would be if Abby didn't seem to care about Jessie. But she did.

So the only obstacle to a serious relationship with Abby was Abby herself. Not because he didn't think she felt the same way he did. But because nine years ago, he'd made her lose trust in herself.

And that was something not so easily fixed. She'd spent years thinking she'd made a grave error in judgment. That mind-set would take time and patience to overcome.

It looked like the next weeks could prove to be very very interesting. And hopefully life-changing for both of them.

Chapter Seven

The next morning, Abby walked hesitantly toward Colin and Jessie's door. She'd dreaded facing him since fleeing the porch the night before; consequently, she hadn't gotten much sleep. She'd finally drifted off when the first streaks of daybreak began to lighten the sky. Her alarm had dragged her out of her restless sleep not two hours later.

Taking a deep breath, she tried to settle her nerves. "This is ridiculous," she muttered. "He's just a man."

A man who kissed you senseless last night, an errant voice quipped in her head. *A man you kissed back,* it added.

Abby knocked on Number Ten's door harder than

she'd meant to, trying to drown out her thoughts. In the next instant the door flew open.

"Abby!" Jessie shrieked, and plowed into her, pressing her cheek into Abby's lower abdomen in a fierce hug.

Only her nephew Jamie greeted her with such enthusiasm. Had her efforts to live a circumspect life and keep her emotions contained pushed the rest of her family away? Remembering the way she'd needled Sam when her budding relationship with Nic Verdini landed her on the front pages of several tabloids, Abby thought perhaps she had. Sam might have needed a hug from her sister, not criticism.

Abby shut her eyes, enjoying Jessie's embrace and fighting the tears that welled up. She could only blame them on lack of sleep. Once again, admitting that the life she'd chosen had left her battling loneliness was unthinkable.

"I was hoping to run into you," Colin said softly into her ear.

When he took her arm, a thrilling jolt of electricity shot through her. Her thoughts scattered and she felt herself blush as she let him draw her farther into the room.

She'd meant to tell them about the need to switch rooms and quickly retreat, Abby remembered belatedly. But Colin was talking again before she could gather her wits to tell him about the room switch. "I promised to take Jessie to a movie, and I'd hoped you'd come along. I thought we'd stop for dinner somewhere along the way, too."

She was shaking her head before she could even

process all the reasons she had to say no. Before old wants and needs could tempt her further, "I can't," she said. Not *no*. Not *I don't want to*. Not even *Not if you were the last man on earth*. Just the bald truth. *I can't.*

"Please-oh-please, Abby," Jessie begged, gaining Abby's attention. Her brown eyes bright with hope and just a tinge of desperation as she hopped up and down.

Abby could have cheerfully strangled Colin when she looked back up at him. The sparkle in his eyes and his easy smile said he knew, damn him, that she didn't want to disappoint Jessie. "Yeah, please, Abby," Colin echoed softly.

"Why?" she asked, forgetting Jessie's presence as the sparkle in his eyes changed to a sexy twinkle.

"Because *I* want you to come." He glanced down at Jessie. "I'll explain why later if you really need me to."

What she needed was to get out of there. "I'll think about it," she said, refusing to be cornered while she contemplated his motives.

What could he want? It had to be about Torthúil Acres or Gardens or whatever his silly development was supposed to be called. Believing anything else would be just plain stupid. And Abby wasn't stupid.

Not anymore.

"I came up to tell you that I need to move you to another room," she said, determined to get her errand over with and get back to her life. She didn't mind providing a fairy-tale room for a child, but a long time ago Abby had faced the very real truth that there wouldn't be any storybook ending for her—ever.

"I have this specific room promised to a couple scheduled to arrive today. I readied another room for you earlier this morning," she said and pointed down the hall. "I gave you Number Seven. There's a big bedroom, plus small room off the other side of the bath. I thought you could use it when Jessie goes to bed. It's set up like a sitting room but it has a Murphy bed and a television."

He narrowed his eyes. "You're giving us a suite?"

She huffed out a breath. Was he implying that she'd soak his bank account to punish him for the mistakes of the past? "The price will stay the same."

Colin sighed quietly but she heard his impatience even before he said, "I can afford more, Abby, and I wasn't hinting that you were trying to overcharge me. I was just surprised you'd have a suite unreserved and I don't want to have to continue to uproot Jessie every day or so when you have that room promised to someone else."

"The turret room isn't specifically reserved again till fall. I just finished redecorating it. Hopefully you'll have Torthúil more than livable for Jessie by then."

Colin gave her a sharp nod. "We'll pack, then be down for breakfast."

Abby nodded back and stepped into the hall. "Enjoy your new room, Jessie."

Abby glanced up when Colin and Jessie approached her office an hour later. She set aside the prototypes for her campaign posters as she watched Jessie skip ahead of Colin, her eyes bright, her feet dancing. Abby grinned and switched her attention from child to adult. Colin looked pensive, as if he was working out a problem.

But he wasn't so deep in thought that he forgot to remind his child of old-fashioned manners Colleen and Liam McCarthy had taught him. Just before Jessie would have come skipping into the office, Colin restrained her with a hand he clamped gently on her shoulder. "What do we do before we go blowing into someone's office and interrupting them?" he asked, hiding a smile.

Jessie sighed as if to say *Manners are just such a bother*. Which left Abby hiding a grin, too.

"We knock," the newly crowned princess of the tower said with a dramatic sigh.

"And if the door already happens to be open?" Colin prodded.

"We say, escuse me. Escuse me, Miss Abby," she said, and she rapped her little knuckles on the doorjamb then rubbed them against her T-shirt. "Can I come in?"

Abby could see Jessie, in every fiber of her being, was bursting to tear in no doubt with the sole purpose of talking Abby's ear off.

Abby grinned. "I'd love the company," she told Jessie. "How do you like your room?"

Jessie was across the room and rounding the desk in the blink of an eye. She wrapped her arms around Abby's neck and squeezed. "Oh, it's won'erful. I asked Daddy if I can have a room just like it at Torthúil."

"And what did Daddy say?" Abby asked, curious how Colin would feel about Jessie's admiration for the design. He didn't tend to dress her like a girl. How would he feel about so feminine a style taking over in a corner of his house?

Colin perched on the side of her desk next to her as he answered, and her senses went on alert thanks to his nearness. "Daddy said he could handle the cornice and painting the walls, but he'd have to enlist the help of a decorator for the colors and fabrics." He grinned down at Abby. "I seem to remember someone who'd planned to go into that line of work."

This was simply too close for comfort—both physically and emotionally. He had remembered her dreams. Dreams she'd altered and kissed goodbye when other things like, first, survival and then saving Hopewell Manor took priority.

Even as a child, she'd had a passion for decorating. She remembered when her grandparents moved out and her mother was free to put her stamp on the manor. It had been Abby, not yet in school full-time, who'd accompanied her to fabric shops, antique shops and the upholsterers. Juliana had always asked Abby's opinion. To a five-year-old it had been magical to see her choices materialize into furniture, cushions, draperies or wall coverings. She'd been eleven when she'd bought paint and material for Tracy's bedroom as a birthday gift. Mrs. McCarthy had let them paint while she made draperies and bedspreads.

And Colin remembered.

"I've been asking myself whatever happened to that girl," he went on when Abby didn't respond.

Abby pushed her chair away from him, and was tempted to pull Jessie into her hap. But she couldn't use the child like a shield even though she desperately needed some breathing room.

Even so, she also wanted to answer truthfully. After what her father had done to Colin, he deserved to know about the debacle James Hopewell's life had become.

She picked up the pile of her campaign brochures she had ready for the mail. "Jessie, would you like to help me? There's a box on the porch under the mail box. Could you put these in it for me?

Jessie nodded and grinned broadly, clearly thrilled to help.

Once she was out of earshot, Abby said, "Huge changes happened. My father went out on his boat in spite of storm warnings, but he didn't go alone. He took his new wife and two other couples to their deaths with him. Their families filed a lawsuit that drained our father's estate, leaving only Sam's and my college trust funds and Hopewell Manor untouched. We had to support ourselves as well as handle the upkeep on the manor. Mama had this land she'd bought with her divorce settlement and she'd been quietly looking into starting up a winery. We all got behind her and her idea. Sam was already in agricultural school. I was a sophomore by then so I changed my major to what we needed me to learn—hotel management. Caro had just graduated with a degree in business management and Mama found a vintner to help get things started. The rest is history."

"My brother-in-law, Ed—he married my sister Mary—told me about your parent's divorce and your dad's death. He also mentioned some financial problems surrounding his death, but that was all the update I ever got."

"Erin was here last year," Abby told him. "I'm surprised she didn't fill you in about the winery and Cliff Walk at least. She even stayed here."

"Erin always loved you. It doesn't surprise me that she'd stop to see you on her way through the area. But your family was a sore subject for me and they all know it. Neither I nor my parents told them why. Around me there was just an unspoken rule not to bring up Hopetown let alone the Hopewell name. When they visited Jess and me in California, Mary spent the whole time shooting daggers at Ed for even telling me what he did."

Abby chuckled as Jessie skipped back in and climbed into her lap. The oldest of the McCarthy kids, Mary had always been a force to be reckoned with. "Remember the day we played house in her graduation dress?"

Colin snorted. "Why am I surprised the roof leaks? Mary about blew it off that day with all her screaming."

"How Aunt Mary could blow off a roof, Daddy? Like the big bad wolf did?"

Jessie's innocent query startled Abby. She'd grown

so comfortable she'd nearly forgotten the child was in her lap. How could she have become so at ease with Colin that she'd been joking with him? Reliving old memories with him?

"...so it's just an old saying," she heard Colin saying, once some of Abby's shock wore off. "It means Aunt Mary was very angry at your aunt Tracy and Abby and she shouted a lot."

"Aunt Mary's always mad at somebody," Jessie said, and waved her hand in a very adult gesture, further dismissing her aunt's moods.

Colin pursed his lips, clearly fighting a grin. "That's not nice, Jess. Aunt Mary is family. And an adult. I expect you to respect her and that means not saying mean things about her. Now, why don't you go out to the kitchen and ask Genevieve for the lunch she promised to pack for us?"

After another quick hug and thanks for the princess room, Jessie—her safety net—was gone. Again, Colin wasted no time at all getting to the point. A point that scared Abby witless since he apparently could read her mind.

"Abby, there's nothing wrong with revisiting old times. We share some very good ones. That's why I want you to go with us tonight. We have too much in common to avoid each other the way we've been." He held her gaze steadily. "And we have too much attraction going on between us to try pretending it doesn't exist. We need to figure out why, after nine years, the sparks still fly when we're near each other."

"No, we don't. *I* don't." She turned toward her desk and picked up the posters, pretending to study them, determined to ignore his presence.

He ran his finger up her neck and her traitorous body shivered with delicious yearning. He bent toward her ear, his warm breath stirring her hair. It was every bit as exciting as his touch. "I notice you didn't deny the sparks."

"It just wouldn't work. We're on opposite sides of what promises to be a huge and ugly fight." She slanted the poster more in his direction and tapped it. "I'm running for mayor, Colin," she said, and put the poster back on the stack. "You see what an opportunist Harley Bryant is. He has to be ousted from office and a lot of people feel I'm the one who can do it. We can't be seen together. It could be misinterpreted as a conflict of interest for me."

"Abby, you can't live your life by what people may or may not think." Colin looked down at her and, though he smiled, she could see the intent look in his eyes.

She clasped her hands in her lap and pushed back away from her desk—away from him. She had to make him understand, and getting distracted by his nearness was only going to get in her way. "You weren't here after my father destroyed our lives with his affair. You didn't hear the whispers. Deal with the gossip. Then there was his death. The Hopewell name was suddenly nothing but fodder for sensational gossip. I won't knowingly go there again."

"Suppose I tell anyone with the nerve to ask that you only went along because I promised to give you a chance to change my mind."

She felt hopeful suddenly. It wasn't as if her concerns about the river were frivolous. Maybe she could change his mind. "Will you?"

Colin pursed his lips, crossed his ankles and folded his arms, hoping he looked nonchalant and not uptight. She wasn't going to give up trying to stop the development, but he wasn't giving up on it, either. Too much was riding on the success of Torthúil Gardens. His every dream. His every goal. And then there was his promise to fulfill his father's dream of the homestead surviving for generations to come. "There's more to the development than putting money in my pocket," he told her.

"And there's more going on with the river than Harley Bryant probably led you to believe. If you'd been here in the spring you'd—"

"Okay," Colin broke in. "We'll talk about it. I'll hear you out. That's the best I can promise." He doubted that she could say anything to deter him, though.

"So what's the movie?" she asked. It wasn't total victory for him, he thought, but better than an outright refusal.

Colin grinned. "I'm the father of a four-year-old. Don't expect too much." And he'd better not expect too much either, he cautioned himself.

Abby smiled. "I'll have you know, I love cartoons and G-rated movies. I have a nephew, remember? And Caro has a baby girl she's pretty busy with right now. As does Sammie, so I've become the official movie and a burger auntie."

"I think I can do better than a burger and fries," Colin protested.

"I'm sure you can, but you don't need to. Jessie would probably rather have—"

"Miss Genevieve says we should have a nice day," Colin heard Jessie huff out from the doorway. He pivoted a bit to see her dragging the cooler along the slick hardwood hall floor. "There's an awful lot of food in here," she declared and stood straight, looking at Abby. "Maybe you could come too and help us eat it. And maybe before, we could go for a walk while Daddy works. And maybe you could show me all the places at Torthúil where you played. And maybe—"

"Hold it, Jess," Colin cut in. While he hadn't minded letting Jess con Abby into dinner and a movie, he didn't want Abby feeling too much pressure from the two of them. "Abby has work to do just like I do."

Jessie looked at her shoes—an utterly pathetic creature—all hopes dashed. "Oh."

"I can't, honey," Abby said, sounding genuinely disappointed. "I have new customers checking in today and early this evening. But I am going to dinner and a movie with you some night soon."

Jessie brightened. "You are?" She stabbed her fist in the air. "Yes! We'll have lots of fun. I can hardly wait!"

Abby smiled. "Me, either."

Jessie skipped up to the other side of Abby's desk, leaned her forearms on the top and her chin on her fists and groaned. "It's just going to be so…o…o boring today. Do I really hafta stay on the porch at Torthúil all day again?" she asked, tilting her head to gaze up at him with puppy-dog eyes.

Colin gave her his standard you-know-the-answer-to-that look. Her bottom lip pouted out so he knew she got the message, but Abby wasn't quite on to his daughter and her acting ability.

"You know, I have an idea," Abby said brightly. "Why don't you stay here with me today, Jessie? That way you can help me around here and your daddy can concentrate on his work."

"No, Ab. I can't ask—" he began.

"You didn't ask. I did," Abby said in a no-nonsense tone he still had trouble equating with the girl he'd once known. But then she'd faced more adversity in the years he'd been gone than he would have thought the daughter of a wealthy, prominent family had in store for her.

"Please, Daddy. Please," Jessie begged. She'd be on her knees pretty soon if he didn't agree.

"I was over at the house with Erin in the spring," Abby put in before he could concede defeat. "You know you don't really want to have Jessie there again until you're comfortable with the house's safety. Besides, maybe you'll get more done this way."

He hated to admit it but she was right. Yesterday, it had felt as if he'd spent most of his time running up and down the stairs checking on Jess. He was terrified something on four legs would come crawling out from somewhere and encounter her. And Jessie, little earth mother that she was, would be tempted to make a friend rather than call him for a rescue.

"It would be a help," he admitted, not wanting to sound too eager for the help. Then he nodded a bit toward Jessie. "The exterminator's due today so if you're sure you wouldn't mind..."

Abby's eyes narrowed a bit when she said, "I wouldn't have suggested it otherwise." Then she looked away and smiled at his daughter. "We'll have fun, won't we, Jessie?"

He wanted his child safe. And to be honest, Abby's feminine influence on his little tomboy wouldn't hurt to smooth out some of her rough edges. But Jessie's eager defection stung a little. Not really wanting to leave either of them, Colin hauled himself to his feet. Enough stalling. He had a full day ahead ripping out water-damaged plaster, rotted timbers and maybe helping the exterminator with his grim task.

He looked at Abby smiling at Jess and smiled, too. This move back to Hopetown might turn out to be the best one he'd ever made.

Chapter Eight

Clasped hands swinging between them, Abby and Jessie strolled down Torthúil's private lane. Jessie strutted slightly, proud of the little green sundress she wore. Abby had picked it up on their trip to the mall that morning. They'd gone after Abby checked in all her new guests and said a quick farewell to the departing ones.

Abby smiled. She grew more and more attached to Colin's daughter each day she spent with her. She seemed to fill the empty spot in her heart Abby had only begun to acknowledge. A week had gone by and each day Colin left Jessie behind no less reluctantly than that first one. Abby really thought he missed his daughter more than she missed him, which was kind of sweet.

But it wasn't safe to see anything about Colin McCarthy as sweet.

Which was why she'd continued trying to avoid him. It was nearly impossible, though, because if she managed it, he'd do something like what he'd done yesterday. He'd sent her flowers to thank her for Jessie's princess room at Cliff Walk.

No one had ever sent her flowers before.

When she'd managed to avoid him for two straight days, he'd sent her candy—the dark chocolates she loved. Somehow he'd remembered those were her favorite.

She'd told herself he fought dirty. But she hadn't realized how dirty until Jessie handed her a personally constructed invitation to this picnic lunch. Now how was she supposed to say no to that?

Which was why she was walking along Torthúil's cracked-granite driveway hand in hand with Jessie. The driveway led past the once bountiful orchards—cherry trees to the left and pear and apple to the right. Now the trees stood, still vividly green but wild and untamed. Their condition made her a little sad.

They came next to what Abby believed was the most beautiful part of the farm, the leafy tunnel formed by ancient oaks, marching like soldiers along both sides of the driveway shading and guarding the entrance to the heart of Torthúil.

The house.

The home.

As it came into view, Abby was struck by the heart-breaking fact that the house, once so filled with love that she'd thought of it as a second home, now stood empty. Derelict. The porch where she'd played house, hospital, then finally Miss America looked fragile, as if, without the temporary added bracing Colin must have added, the next storm would blow it away.

The bright lemon-yellow paint had peeled, revealing the white of a previous generation. Other clapboards had peeled clear to the bare wood. Most of the shutters hung crookedly, their once-vibrant green faded and chalky.

It was so near to a perfect symbol of her sad, empty life it was downright terrifying. And that was never more clear to her than it was each night after Colin returned to Cliff Walk for a shower and dinner and the evening with Jessie. He always asked her to join them for a walk or in front of the TV in their room, but Abby, of course, always turned him down.

She'd had plenty of time to absorb everything he'd told her the night of the zoning board meeting. Now that she understood why it had all happened, it hurt even more. She'd been banished from Torthúil—tried, convicted and sentenced—without a trial. Her character had meant nothing. They'd all believed the worst. The pain of knowing her father—the hero of her childhood—had betrayed her so completely was made worse by the knowledge that it really had been all her fault. She had surrendered to her feelings—her passionate longing for Colin—and lost nearly everything she'd cared about.

Everywhere she looked, memories bombarded her. That they were all good ones made the urge to cry stronger and stronger the closer they got to the house. Abby wished she'd driven. It hadn't been like this with Erin at her side last spring. Walking simply gave her too much time to think, too much time to remember.

A hot breeze blew in off the river, ruffling her skirt and a few stray strands of hair that escaped the clip she'd used to pile it on top of her head. She breathed in the smell of moss and newly cut wood. Even the smell of Torthúil was different now.

Everything was different.

Jessie pointed far off toward the river. "Is that the barn where you and Aunt Tracy hid from Aunt Mary when she wrecked the roof?"

Abby chuckled. "You mean when we played in her dress. Yes. That's the one. It's where your father found us and told your grandparents where we were, too. Your gram came out and lectured us about touching your aunt Mary's dress. But then she asked us to stay hidden so your aunt Mary would learn a lesson, too. So we stayed and your daddy brought us lunch and dinner, too."

Jessie's nose wrinkled in thought. "What she teached Aunt Mary?"

To Abby's way of thinking, Mary's had really been the greatest lesson of the day. Abby squatted down to Jessie's height. "She learned that things aren't as important as people. She was very worried when she thought we'd run away because of all her shouting."

Jessie nodded sagely, but her quick young mind skittered off in a new direction. She tugged on the quilt Abby had brought along. "Is this old as you?"

Abby chuckled again and stood as another breeze stirred the air. "No. I made this out of some old dresses."

"When this is old could you put it in a quilt for me?" Jessie twirled around, clearly thrilled with her new dress.

Abby herself wore a similar dress in deference to the ninety-degree day. It wasn't the way she usually dressed, so she was a bit unsure of herself. But Jessie had seen it in the window of a shop and had so desperately wanted them to dress alike for this picnic that Abby hadn't had the heart to refuse. Like Jessie's, it was a soft green with darker sprigs of green sprinkled across the hemline. It was more revealing than Abby was used to, leaving her shoulders bare except for a thin pair of straps.

A stamping sound from above drew their attention as they walked up a slight rise toward the house. Colin stood alone, balanced on the stripped roof, shooting nails into new roof sheathing. He waved and they both waved back, then he pointed to the last oak tree. Jessie shrieked and ran back to a brand-new wooden swing that hung from a lower branch by bright-blue nylon ropes. Shouting her thanks, she jumped on, tiptoeing to give herself a push.

Colin laughed and yelled, "You're welcome," then went back to work.

It was a good thing Jessie was occupied with her swing and Colin with his work because she stood transfixed by the sight of him. He was stripped to the waist, strong and lithe as he finished fastening down the large roof section with the air gun. Only when he disappeared inside was Abby able to shake loose of the mesmerizing sight.

Why don't you just drool, Abby? admonished the voice in her head.

"Push me, Abby. Push me!" Jessie called.

Glad of the distraction, Abby dropped the quilt on the grass at the edge of the driveway and went to do just that. Several minutes later she heard a scuffing sound and looked over at the porch. Colin and two lanky youths walked across the porch toward the steps. He handed each of them some money and clapped one on the back.

The boys leaped over the shaky railing and jumped on their bikes, giving her the prodding she needed to look away from Colin. She followed the boys' progress as they tore up the driveway. She recognized one of them. Her sister Samantha and their vintner, Will Reiger, often hired him to help out at the vineyard.

"The blond guy's a real go-getter," Colin said from next to her. His musky scent enveloped her, tuning up her awareness of him. "His buddy needs watching," he went on, seemingly unmindful of the effect his nearness had on her suddenly thundering heart. "Got to hand it to Greg, he handled him for me and kept him hustling."

"Ha-handled what?" she asked, distracted and not following his line of thought.

"His friend was goofing off, but Greg handled it before I needed to. He'll make a great foreman someday. I may bring them back."

"Greg is Henry Chaffee's son," she told him. "He's been showing up on our doorsteps looking for work since he was twelve."

Colin looked puzzled. "I didn't connect the last name. I could have sworn Henry went on to law school after college."

She continued to force her attention on pushing Jessie, to keep her eyes off Colin. It was an act of supreme self-control but then, after giving Jessie another push, she weakened and let her eyes stray his way.

He'd doused himself with water and there were still droplets on his golden shoulders and sparkling in the dark hair sprinkled lightly across his chest. She'd never seen anything as sexy as the droplet that rolled down the valley between those six-pack abs and into his navel. Unless it was the way the water-darkened waistband of his jeans rode low on his hips.

She looked away and cleared her throat, forcing herself to concentrate on the underlying message behind what he'd said about Greg. There'd been something annoying about his comment. Then she realized what. "You're a snob, Colin McCarthy," she accused him.

He looked dumbfounded. "What?"

"Henry Chaffee has a very successful legal practice. But if Greg wants video games or a high-end bike like the one he just rode off on, he has to earn the money for it. Henry's trying to instill his work ethic and respect for money in his kids no matter how easy life could be for them."

Colin's chin notched up and he yanked on his T-shirt. "How the hell can I be a snob when this is what I come from?" he demanded, gesturing around them.

"Because you seem to think manual labor is beneath certain people and not others. Admit it, you're appalled that I clean and make the beds at Cliff Walk. Here's a flash, I also scrub the toilets and do the laundry. Do I care if you still swing a hammer and haul debris on job sites? No."

"Are you guys fighting?" Jessie asked.

"Of course we aren't fighting," Colin lied smoothly. "Abby just doesn't understand something Daddy said. I'll explain it and everything will be okay. Now quit conning her. You can pump that swing yourself. You play over here for a few minutes while we get lunch set up, then we'll eat. Okay?"

"Sure, Daddy," Jessie agreed then leaned back and reached out with her feet to set the swing flying higher than Abby had pushed her.

"We'll call you when lunch is all set," Colin promised again. He pivoted, scooped up the quilt and the cooler she hadn't even noticed till then and walked toward the tree off to the right of the house. Abby had little choice but to follow.

Surrounded by sunshine, the elm sat alone with no trees within a hundred yards on any side. It was probably the only reason it hadn't fallen victim to Dutch elm disease. Beneath it lay a thick carpet of grass that had been freshly mowed. Colin had been busy.

"I thought this tree would be long gone," he said, looking up into the lush canopy.

"Don't change the subject. You told Jessie you'd explain," she challenged.

Colin deftly snapped the quilt in the air and settled it neatly. Then he knelt and sat back on his heels, pulling the cooler in front of him to unload it. "I'm not a snob, but I get what you mean. I guess I'm having trouble with the way the social order here has been scrambled around."

"Colin, except for the Bryant family holding on for dear life to the *social order*, there isn't one."

"Don't give me that. You're as hung up on the Hopewell name as any Bryant ever was."

Abby sank to the blanket. The man was utterly exasperating. "The name, not our social standing. Our house is on the Historical Register. There's an iron plaque by the road that the government put there. Over three hundred years ago one of my ancestors started that town. I'm proud of our history. Your ancestors came here and built Torthúil over a hundred years ago. That's something to be proud of, too."

She wanted him to understand. She really did. "Colin, there won't be any more Hopewells after I'm gone. You weren't here when my father did his midlife-crisis thing. People died because of him. I just want the Hopewells to be remembered for more than that."

Colin's eyes narrowed. "So you've given up all your dreams to make up for what he did."

She shook her head. "I love my work. And Cliff Walk. I enjoy making people's experiences here good ones."

"The day we moved rooms you lugged our baggage from one room to another by yourself," he countered. "I could have done that. I never wanted you as a servant, Ab. I admit I wished your father would have lived to feel powerless, the way he made me and my parents feel the day he threatened to destroy our home. But I never thought of what that would do to the rest of you."

"Your wishes didn't make anything happen. My father's mistakes did. What we're doing—the vineyard, the winery, Cliff Walk—it's good. We don't have the bank account we once did, but compared to some others in this world we're doing pretty good. Yes, we started from a desperate place. Mama was only supposed to be allowed to stay at Hopewell Manor until I graduated college, then my father and his new wife were slated to move in.

"Mama didn't share her dream of the winery with us, but then Father died, and we were all in the same boat. I'd like to think we'd all be doing exactly what we are even if my father had lived. I think we'd have stuck by Mama's dream and worked to make it a reality."

"Are you saying he'd have been okay with the winery?"

Abby let out an unladylike snort. "Get real. He'd be having conniptions seeing Sammie farm and me running Cliff Walk!"

"See?"

"No. *You* see. For *him* it was about his standing in the social order. But I'm not my father. I just don't want my family to be remembered as a bad joke."

Colin looked at Abby's upturned face, wanting more than anything to kiss her and hold her. When she was near him it was a struggle to keep his mind on the important things like developing an understanding of her and the life she'd built.

She was right. She wasn't at all like her father, even though she was the only daughter who resembled him. But he wasn't *his* father, either. He would never let himself be put in a position where Jessie's happiness could be destroyed by someone bent on controlling him with his finances. Once his plans came to fruition, he'd be the one on top. And once he was there, he'd be a hell of a lot better to people than James Hopewell had ever been. Maybe it was time he shared the rest of his plans with her.

"I wanted to let you know that Torthúil Gardens isn't the only iron I have in the fire. I bid on a construction company. It's in trouble and the owner wants out. It'll give me enough equipment and manpower to move forward on the house and eventually the project here."

She nodded, appearing a little sad as she looked over toward the house.

He guessed he and Abby would just have to agree to disagree about the project. It wouldn't matter anyway. Seeing her here cemented it all in his mind. She was back where she belonged. "Abby, let's not let Torthúil Gardens come between us. Stop hiding from me. Let's just spend time together and see where it goes. Just you and me. *And* Jessie," he added with a laugh as he heard her chattering to herself on the swing.

He looked his daughter's way and noticed she wore a dress, not the camp shorts he'd given her to put on that morning. And it wasn't her one and only dress, either. He started to wonder how he'd missed that but then he realized Abby had captured his attention and distracted him from Jess. That had never happened before.

"Speaking of my daughter, did she con you into a shopping trip?"

"More like I dragged her along. I wanted to pick up some clothes for Sam and Caro's girls. Jessie admired the dress."

"So you bought it for her? It's enough that you're watching her so I can get more done."

"She wanted to wear a dress, but the one she had didn't say picnic or…well…it wasn't exactly Jessie."

"No, it was Erin. She sent it for Easter. It's a little too 'poufy,' Jess called it. Thanks."

"You're both welcome. So what's for lunch?"

He lifted the lid of the cooler Genevieve had packed for them and looked inside. He couldn't hold back a smile. This didn't look much like the sandwich lunch he'd asked for. He pulled out a bottle of Hopewell's Pinot Grigio. A sliced baguette. Brie. Smoked salmon pâté. Then strawberries and chocolate sauce—dark-chocolate sauce. And a peanut butter sandwich, chocolate soy milk and cookies.

Abby's cook was matchmaking.

And he didn't mind a bit.

He glanced at Abby. A blush stained her cheeks when she looked down and zeroed in on the romantic lunch he'd pulled out of the cooler. "Oh, God! What was she thinking! I'll kill her. Honestly. Will Jessie even eat Brie?"

Colin shook his head. "Nope. She says it looks like snot."

Abby choked, then laughed.

He loved hearing her laugh and was glad he'd gotten her to relax enough to let it out. "What can I say? My child's got no taste. There's a lunch just for Jess, too. Your Genevieve is nothing if not efficient."

"Efficient? She's a menace," Abby grumbled, but started spreading some salmon on a piece of the baguette then bit into it with her straight white teeth. He stared as she closed her eyes and let out a little groan. His pulse sped up and things south of his belt buckle stirred to life. He shook his head and looked away to pour the wine into the wineglasses the efficient Genevieve had sent along.

He sat back on his heels and took a moment to enjoy the sight of Abby again. Her hair was piled on top of her head and her slender neck lay exposed, tempting him. He leaned forward and kissed that vulnerable spot, the little knob where her neck ended and her back began. It was delicious.

And she shivered in spite of the heat and stared at him with widened emerald eyes when he pulled back. He couldn't hold back a pleased smile—nor was he able to look away.

"You shouldn't do that. Jessie might see. It might confuse her," Abby said, her voice hushed, a little breathless.

"Jessie is fine. She's crazy about you. I've taken a backseat to someone for the first time in her life."

She looked instantly guilty. "I never meant to replace—"

"Hey, relax," he broke in. "She's acting like a little girl for a change. I sometimes worry that I've embraced her inner tomboy a bit too much. She looks really cute today. It's fine that she wants to be with you." And he knew it was. He wanted to spend time with Abby too.

He looked around and didn't see the farm the way it was now but the way it had been. And the way it would be. It was cathartic to spend so much time there after being forced to leave. It had begun to feel like home already. And it felt right to have Abby there at Torthúil. And knowing it felt right made him sure there was more between them than a shared past and nearly uncontrollable desire on his part.

He'd missed her that week as she ducked him at every opportunity and continued to shy away from him by using Jessie as a shield when she couldn't avoid him altogether. So he'd stepped up the campaign with flowers and candy—a kind he knew she loved. And today Jessie had innocently brought in the big guns with her request for this picnic and her lovingly constructed invitation that Genevieve had helped her put together.

"And speaking of her wanting to be with you," he said, hoping he sounded casual when he was anything but. "If we're going to make good on our promise to take her to dinner and that movie, it really has to be tonight. They aren't showing it anywhere nearby after this. Come on, Ab, say yes. What could one night out hurt? I promised to listen to your objections to the Torthúil Gardens project. This is your chance. I thought you'd be pushing me to pick a night."

"All right," she said on a deep exhalation.

And his heart leaped for joy.

It was as if the old spell Abby had woven around his heart years earlier had been lying dormant, only to spring to life in full bloom when he saw her again. He didn't believe in love at first sight, but he was nearly sure what he felt for her—what he'd always felt for her—was love. He knew without a doubt that she'd always meant more to him than had been wise and she still did. It was no wiser now considering her race for mayor and his stand on the opposite side of a major campaign issue, but at least she was no longer too young for him. Soon, after the housing project was done, he'd have the prestige of wealth to match her prominent name.

They'd be equals at last.

Maybe they could find a future together.

But only if they could find a way to negotiate the rocky present. Tonight, he promised himself. Tonight he'd show her they belonged together.

Chapter Nine

Colin paced Cliff Walk's parlor as he waited for Abby and Jessie. *It's just dinner and a movie,* he told himself, but it felt like more. They'd had a nice time at lunch, but he'd had to get back to work so the roof would be under cover by nightfall. Thunderstorms were once again fore-casted.

He raked a hand through his hair and turned at the sound of footsteps. It wasn't Abby or Jessie but a small blond woman he thought he recognized. She held a tiny baby cradled in her arms.

"You're Samantha. Sammie, right?" he asked. "And that must be, Nikki."

Abby's sister smiled. "Yep. I heard you were back."

He bent down to look closer at the baby. She was

tiny, each feature a miniature of her mother's, except her eyes, which were as dark as chips of polished coal.

"Hello, little one," Colin said. "I see why that dog Jamie's got might have been a bit much for you."

Samantha seemed to assess him for a long moment. "My husband, Nic, went a little American crazy for a while there. 'An American bambina must have a dog. It's a custom, no?'" she said in perfectly affected Italian accent. "We had a chat, Nic and I. And the dog went to Jamie." She smirked but love shone in her eyes for the husband she'd imitated. "Anyway, I'm here for a couple reasons." Her hazel eyes narrowed and, even with the tiny baby in her arms and standing five foot nothing, she looked formidable. "Reason one is to warn you. Don't hurt my sister again."

Colin resisted the urge to step back. "How did you—?"

Samantha held up her hand. "I don't know what happened and I don't want to. That's Abby's business. But she went through hell that year and it started when you blew out of town."

"I've heard. All I can say is I never meant to hurt her. And I'm not here to do it again. I came back to develop Torthúil and fix up the house. Maybe to figure out what was missing from my life," he said, and turned when footsteps echoed in the foyer.

Abby floated in and smiled. She wore her hair down again tonight. He let his eyes feast on her. She looked delicate and ethereal in a gauzy white pants outfit. "And I think I found out what was missing," he muttered.

Only Samantha's snicker made him realize he'd spoken aloud.

"Yeah, you'll do," she said quietly, and he knew her comment was for his ears only. The look in her eyes told him she meant for their entire conversation to stay just as private.

He nodded his agreement and turned to look at Abby. Colin's pulse skittered as he took Abby's hand. She could weave a spell around him by just walking into a room. He had to find some way to make this work. When she explained her concerns tonight about his plans for Torthúil, he'd listen carefully and try to explain how important the project was to him and the town.

Behind him, Samantha cleared her throat and yanked him loose from thoughts again. Colin didn't let Abby's hand go but turned back to face Samantha. She glanced down at their clasped hands and grinned as she went on. "I just stopped by to let you know about the camp I'm running here during August. It starts next week. Runs for two. I know Abby's been keeping an eye on your daughter till it's safe at the farmhouse for her, and I thought you might like to enroll her in the camp. She'd be younger than a lot of the kids who signed up, but there are a couple of five-year-olds. I hired two older kids to help, so we'll keep an eye on them."

"I don't know," he said, and glanced toward Abby. Jessie would love it, but he'd never trusted just anyone with his daughter.

"I noticed your daughter is sort of the rough-and-tumble type in spite of Abby's obvious influence. If you remember anything about me at all, I really get the tomboy thing. We'll do lots of digging and some late-season planting, nature walks, a few art projects. Just drop her off at the winery courtyards around ten."

"You've been getting an earlier start than that over at the house. I could still keep an eye on her till ten and watch her after camp ends," Abby offered.

He'd thought Jess could start coming to the house with him soon. He hardly saw her anymore. Colin felt unaccountable panic. Until leaving her with Abby, not a day had gone by during her entire life that he hadn't stopped several times during the day to see her. He was barely seeing her for three or four hours a day. "I don't know." He hesitated. "She'll be able to play over at Torthúil soon…and I can…"

"Colin," Abby said, and squeezed his hand. "Jessie needs children to play with. She has no friends. From what both of you said about her life in California, she never really has."

Guilt assailed him as he nodded. "But we've been to lots of playgrounds where she's played with kids. She never acted like she missed—"

"Because you can't miss what you never had," Abby jumped in and explained. "She thinks of other children passing on the edge of her life as perfectly normal."

Colin felt like an idiot. And a rotten father. He couldn't seem to get any words out so he just dropped Abby's hand and turned away. His neighborhood in L.A. had been populated with working couples, some families with teens and a few singles—but no children. There was the occasional kid in neighborhoods where the houses were that he worked on but they always got left behind when they moved on to the next job site. And, of course, what Jess called "playground kids," as if she thought parks came equipped with temporary playmates. What kind of idiot didn't notice his kid was lonely?

He felt a hand settle on his back, and Abby's calm serenity seemed to envelop him. "Jessie is the happiest little girl on the planet," she told him. "You've given her something the three of us would have given anything for."

Colin knew she meant her and her two sisters but didn't understand what could possibly have been missing from their lives. They'd had everything any kid could want. He turned back to face Abby and her sister. Hadn't they?

She must have seen the question in his eyes. "You love her unconditionally. That's the best gift any little girl can ask of her father."

"It's something none of us ever got from our father," Samantha added. And as she listed the ways his nemesis had treated his girls, Colin got a sad look into their childhood—one that had him questioning everything he'd heard of their lives from Tracy. Caro had been pressured in academics. Samantha criticized for not being ladylike enough. And Abby, the youngest, had learned by observing how to make her father love her.

Now he understood why she'd worked so hard in school and at being a perfect little lady around her family. And he understood something even sadder. Torthúil had been the only place for Abby to be herself.

Colin wrapped his arm around Abby's waist, offering the same kind of silent comfort she'd just given him. Her scent curled around him, enveloping him in an odd combination of calm and blazing need.

Sam punched his shoulder as if she could read his mind, but Abby didn't seem to notice. Instead, she smiled at him, then reached up and cupped his cheek. "You're exactly what Jessie needs. Of all the people she talks about, you're clearly her star."

Just then little footsteps tramped toward them. "Abby, I reminded Genni about us eating here. She said— Oh! Look at the doll! Can I play with it?" Jessie begged as she skidded to a stop in front of Samantha and Nikki. Then Sam's tiny baby turned her head, smiled and let out a happy squeal. Jessie jumped backward. Her eyes wide, she gasped. "It's real," she said, clearly awed. "Can I hold it?"

"Sure. Jump on up into that armchair," Samantha suggested.

"I don't know about this," Colin protested. Jessie didn't even have a doll. She always picked out play tools like his when they went to the toy store. Guilt once again assailed him. Had he made another mistake? Maybe she'd just been trying to please him.

"...her back just like this," Samantha was saying as she positioned the baby in Jessie's arms. Next to Jess, baby Nikki didn't look so small, but it was just relative to his daughter's petite size.

"I have an idea," Sam said. "Nic's meeting me here for dinner. Why don't you and Abby have dinner on the terrace and leave Jessie in here with us? We can get to know each other so she's more comfortable with camp. After dinner you three can go on to the movie."

Abby really appreciated Sammie suggesting the camp and her help with Colin's guilt. But right then she could have cheerfully strangled her sister. She'd hoped by them staying there Colin wouldn't be able to pick a romantic setting for their meal. After the intimacy of the picnic Genevieve had packed, she'd hoped for a crowded dining room. Jessie had been her ace in the hole to keep his romancing to a minimum.

Not that her presence had helped all that much that afternoon. Abby had still felt the same emotions, but at least she hadn't been as tempted to act on them with their own pint-size chaperone present. But being alone on the secluded terrace at twilight spelled *romance* in capital letters.

She felt her willpower—her control—dissolve whenever he was near. Just look at her, standing there with Colin's arm around her. He got worried or upset and she instinctively reached out to comfort him. But touching him didn't feel comfortable. Not to her.

He made her want more.

Feel more.

Need more.

She was losing it!

Colin was simply too great a danger to her self-control. She couldn't risk making the same mistakes with Colin again.

She wouldn't.

Back in control, she said, "Jessie should eat with us. Colin hardly saw her again today."

Abby tried to step away from him then, but Colin tightened his grip and said, "No. Much as I miss Jess, I think Samantha's idea is a good one." He stared over at Jessie and Nikki. "This would give Jess a chance to get used to Samantha before the camp starts. I'd feel a lot better about her going if Jess has already gotten to know your sister."

Abby's gaze followed his. Sam had gone over and squatted down, talking to Jessie, who was asking all sorts of questions about baby Nikki. She had to chuckle at one particular question when Jessie asked, "Am you a kid or a mom? 'Cause if you're a mom you sure are a little one."

Sam laughed and her husband, Nic, answered from the doorway. "She is certainly Nikki's mama and, yes, she is a little mama," he conceded as he walked into the room, his eyes on Sam. "She also happens to be perfect just the way she is."

It almost hurt to see Sammie and Nic together. Nic worshipped Sammie and daily let her know that he wouldn't change a thing about her. Their love was like a bright shining light. Beautiful, but hard to look at when your eyes were accustomed to darkness. Love had softened Sammie but Abby had always believed her sister's hard shell had been armor against the pain of rejection she'd surely always felt from their father.

Just then the grandfather clock in the foyer struck six, signaling dinner hour at Cliff Walk and breaking the silence that had fallen over the group.

Sammie picked up Nikki, who'd fallen asleep in Jessie's arms, and nestled her into her baby carrier. Jessie continued to whisper a string of questions as she strolled next to Sam and Nic toward the dining room.

"When I said Jessie needed friends, I was thinking about someone smaller than Sammie and bigger than Nikki, but I guess this is a start," Abby admitted ruefully, trying to tell herself this was her chance to change Colin's mind about developing the land. But she didn't hold out much hope. He seemed committed to the project.

They stepped onto the stone patio that overlooked a terrace of vines and the glistening river far, far below. Every time she looked down on it from there at this time of the day, with the sun slanting low yet still bouncing off the flowing water, the river reminded her of a lovely blue satin ribbon alive in its beauty. But everyone who lived or worked next to it knew it had the ability to morph into a beast.

Beautiful.

Deceptive.

Treacherous.

She loved it and she hated it. Shaking her head in despair, Abby looked away and focused on her immediate surroundings. The table was set with Genevieve's usual attention to detail—and definitely with her more recently acquired interest in romance.

"Hello, you two. Sit. Sit," their own personal middle-aged Cupid said as she bustled out of the kitchen door, carrying two covered plates. The wine had already been poured, the candles already lit. Only two places had been set.

Abby huffed out a breath. "You know, I understand the dining room being full, but we were supposed to have Jessie with us."

"Were you? Imagine me getting my signals crossed like that," she said with a mocking sort of amazement. "Jessie and I had other plans. I'm surprised she didn't tell you. She was so excited. Since Sam and Nic appropriated her, she and I will have our dinner together another night if that's okay with you, Colin."

Abby heard Colin snicker behind her, but when she looked at him he'd schooled his features into a neutral mask. She eyed both of them suspiciously. "Fine. But you wasted your time," she told Genevieve, pointing at her. Then she centered her attention on Colin. "And you promised to listen to me, Colin McCarthy. This is going to be a business dinner whether you like it or not."

"Abby, sit and have a nice meal," Genevieve ordered, but Abby shook her head. Instead she turned away and looked back down at the river, meandering along behind Torthúil's oldest barn. She mentally lined up her argument. Moments later she felt Colin behind her and had to fight to hold on to her agenda and not let his scent and nearness waylay her thoughts.

"It looks so picturesque and innocuous, doesn't it?"

Colin sighed. "Okay, tell me."

Abby leaned forward, intent on making her point. "We had a wet season last summer and it spilled its banks in several places in the fall. The winter wasn't much better and a lot of snow fell across the entire region. Consequently there was a heavier than normal mountain runoff in the spring. Then the last in a series of nor'easters hit us. The river had been swollen already, but that pushed it over its banks. This half of River Road was cut off from everything for two days in both directions. Houses all along the banks for miles sustained damage. Hopewell Manor and Torthúil were spared because of the levees our grandfathers built, but how long those are going to hold out is anyone's guess. Nic got an engineering friend to draw up some plans for a retaining wall between Hopewell Manor's two main building and the levee. Work started just before you arrived."

"So Harley lied about your objections only being about the manor."

"I'm not sure Harley would know the truth if it walked up and bit his butt," she spit out.

She only realized what she'd said when Colin laughed. "He really gets to you, doesn't he?"

Abby crossed her arms. "I don't think I've ever met someone I think less of."

"Then let's not let him ruin our dinner."

She let him guide her to the table, trying not to let the feel of his fingertips resting at the base of her spine distract her, but it wasn't easy. It wasn't any easier when he seated her and kissed her neck again. But she wasn't through with her agenda. "You promised to let me convince you."

Colin grinned. "I promised to let you try." When she glared he sighed. "Abby, I've looked into the flooding. I spoke with the corps of engineers this afternoon. They blame runoff upstream, much farther upstream than Torthúil. And they talked about a massive amount of building that has happened all over the county and throughout the entire watershed region. They aren't looking at one single project as a cause."

He was just like all the others. "Everyone thinks it isn't their project and they're probably right, but someone has to say enough is enough. There's a development out there somewhere that tipped the balance and made things worse in these past two years. How many more will it take to push us completely under?"

"Farming like my parents did it is a thing of the past. As a farm, Torthúil is worthless. It can't survive. I risked my future and Jessie's by buying my sisters out of their shares of the property. Harley assured me that the town needs the tax revenue this project would bring. Was he wrong?"

She wished she could say he was, but the schools were overcrowded and needed upgrading to keep students up with technology. And the roads needed work. She shook her head, feeling defeated. "I get all that, Colin. I really do. But does the project have to be as massive as you explained at the meeting?"

"Abby, I made a promise at my father's grave that I'd find some way to hold on to Torthúil in some form for future generations. And I won't kid you. I also made a promise to myself the day your father walked out of our house after threatening us—that I wouldn't ever be poor again. That I wouldn't have my future or my kids' future in someone else's hands. Surely you can understand why I feel that way."

She could only nod again. What could she say? Her father's legacy marched ever onward. And this time he might have a hand in destroying the town his family founded. Over three hundred years of history could well be washed away because James Hopewell had needed to throw his weight around.

"The land *will* be developed, Ab," Colin went on. "If not by me then by someone else. Someone who won't care at all. Progress means housing. I'm not a reckless person, and I know what I'm doing. I can do what I came here to do and not cause more problems."

Abby was still stuck on his quest for wealth that her father's actions had begun. "How much money will be enough for you?"

He frowned a little considering her question, as if it was one he'd never really thought about before. Finally he said, "I don't know. I was comfortable with my success in California, but it was a rat race and I hadn't built the company to a level where I could move us to a place as rural as Hopetown. So I came back here with a plan. While I want my daughter to grow up here, I don't want her to do it as one of the poor kids the way I did."

"Many people have it a lot worse. Your parents gave you a good life."

Colin nodded. "But I want her to have what you did." He shook his head. "No, that's not right. After just hearing you and Samantha talk about your home life, I want her to have more. The material goods and financial security you had *and* the unconditional love I did."

Abby sat back and picked up her fork. There seemed nothing to do but take a bite of Genevieve's excellent beef bourguignon and ponder her next move. She found Colin's drive for success less annoying knowing his reason was to give Jessie the things he'd missed in his own childhood.

But there had to be another way to achieve it.

Chapter Ten

Abby dropped her head back on the porch swing and inhaled the sultry scents of the hot summer night, waiting for Colin to finish putting Jessie to bed.

As a child, Abby had always loved summer. The sun. The heat. The freedom. No school. Just tubing on the river. Sneaking swims with Tracy. Picnics on the lawn and dinners on the rear terrace of the manor or on the back porch at Torthúil. Those summers had been magical.

She'd spent the past several years practically hiding in the air-conditioned comfort of Cliff Walk. But she'd been a fool to convince herself that she preferred it that way. She'd been a fool to let bad memories rob her of her favorite time of the year.

Little by little, day by day, living with the truth of what had happened that long-ago summer had eased the anguish she'd feel every year as summer heated up.

But there was still a void in her life. She'd be going along just fine and then, from one second to the next, an empty feeling would suddenly descend on her. She had no real emotional anchor.

Her sisters had their husbands, and even her mother seemed to be moving toward forgiving Will Reiger, Hopewell's vintner, for keeping the truth of his wealthy background from them. Poor Will had fallen in love with Juliana at first sight and would not give up on trying to win her heart. But Mama was stubborn and, Abby thought, as afraid as Abby was to trust in love again.

Abby didn't blame her one bit. But this evening with Colin and Jessie had given her a glimpse of what her life could be like if only she had the luxury of being able to throw caution to the wind, embrace her feelings and not fear them.

She'd nearly fooled herself that she could do exactly that until Colin headed down the last hill into Hopetown after the movie. That's when he'd suggested they stop in town for ice cream. Jessie had cheered the idea but, though Abby had wanted to prolong the evening, she'd panicked. All she'd been able to think about was how seeing them together would look to anyone who'd seen or heard about their face-off at the zoning meeting. So she'd suggested they wait for ice cream till they reached Cliff Walk, promising Jessie a first-class sundae.

Jessie, easygoing child that she was, promptly agreed, but Abby had seen the look on Colin's face. He thought she was a coward.

She wasn't. She was just so tired of second-guessing every decision, every action. Public and private. It had simply been easier to come straight home.

And who was he to judge her, anyway? He hadn't lived her life. He hadn't lost the things she had. Confidence in her own judgment—that was the first and most important loss. And knowing that her father had caused all the pain she'd blamed on Colin only added to the toll her father's sins had taken. And it had added Colin to the list of people whose lives her actions had either destroyed or twisted.

Suddenly Colin materialized before her. "Jess dropped off to sleep," he told her, smiling.

Seeing Colin's smile, so full of love for his child, was nearly as hard to look at as seeing Nic and Sammie together. She wanted someone to hold. And someone to hold her.

Thinking of Jessie and Colin sitting across from her chowing down on ice cream, hot fudge and whipped cream, she smiled. "I'm not surprised. She was fading halfway through her ice cream."

"She wanted you to tuck her in. She's crazy about you, Ab. Listen, that nice couple in Ten offered to listen for her, if I wanted to take a walk. I gave them my cell number to call if there's a problem." He glanced out toward the full moon. "What do you say? The moon's bright enough tonight that we wouldn't even need a flashlight."

Abby nodded and stood. A walk sounded like a perfect diversion. As they passed the bed of Colin's truck, he flipped open the big chest where he stored his toolboxes and grabbed the quilt that was still in there from their picnic.

"I wanted to thank you again for all you've done to make Jessie feel at home here," he said, and looped an arm over her shoulders.

Abby's heart stuttered as he moved closer to her and adjusted his stride to hers. *Someone to hold*, she thought again as she put her arm around his waist. Why did it have to feel so good?

"This move by itself had Jess more than a little scared," Colin went on casually as if he hadn't noticed what he did to her equilibrium.

"I know she doesn't seem to think much of the house. But give her time."

"I don't much like the house the way it is now either. It was a pretty huge shock. But Jess had never lived anywhere but our house in L.A. and here I was about to change her world. To calm her down about the move, I gave her a rock I'd carried since the day I left Torthúil. I kept it to remind me of home."

"I'm sorry, Colin," she said automatically, and wondered if the guilt would ever go away.

He stopped and took her by the shoulders. "It's

water under the bridge. No more guilt. We move forward. Deal?"

She wanted to move forward, but didn't know how, or if, she could. Rather than admit that, she changed the subject. "We were talking about the rock you gave her. I don't see how you thought it would help."

He chuckled and took her hand, resuming their walk. "I told her it was a magic rock." Abby laughed. "Hey, it worked for a while. But then we got here and she saw the house. To say she freaked out is putting it mildly. I was desperate the night I arrived on your doorstep. I'd never seen her so inconsolable."

"You have to admit the house is more than a little scary. She talks all the time about an addition you're going to build on it. It's apparently going to be made with rocks like the one you gave her." She grinned. "I assume they'll be a bit bigger than hers. She's anxious to help you pick the rocks."

"Hopefully the phone call I got while I was upstairs will go a long way toward getting closer to that point."

"Oh?"

"It was a call from Ben Warner, the guy selling the company I bid on," he explained.

And Abby's stomach sank. She knew what was coming. Because she was trying to hide her reaction, she nodded and kept walking.

"It was great news," he went on, his voice effervescent with excitement. "Warner accepted my cash bid. It went exactly the way I'd hoped it would."

The night felt suddenly chilly. Involuntarily her

shoulders hunched a little. She hated that she'd hoped the owner would turn down Colin's lowball figure. She should want what was best for him and Jessie, but without manpower or equipment he'd have had to delay his project. "So now you own exactly what?" she asked, not wanting to get into talk about his plans again tonight. She took a deep breath, trying to recapture the peace she'd begun to feel. There was the fragrance of clover and roses on the breeze wafting across the woodlands. The moonlit night lent their surroundings a heavenly magic. It was just too perfect a night to let such earthly concerns intrude.

"I've got enough men and equipment to move forward here. They'll start on the house now so they won't be out of work. I also own the condo development that put Warner under. That's the only part of this that worries me."

"What worries you about those?" She hadn't thought any of this worried him. He always seemed so confident and as if he had it all planned down to the last shingle.

"I have to pull the condo project out of the hole. That's not always easy," he said as they came to a meadow, awash in the silvery light that had illuminated the pathways.

Colin let go of her hand and flipped the blanket open. It settled like a cloud floating to earth. With a smile, he sat in the middle and held his hand out to her. "Be honest, do you really care? Or did you wish I'd lost the bid?"

She sighed and knelt in front of him. Why couldn't

she seem to hide her feelings from him? "Please believe that even though I'm afraid of what will happen if your plans go forward, I also want you to be as successful as you feel you need to be."

He nodded and she settled across from him. "Now, let's talk about something else, Ab. Like why you wouldn't let me stop in town on the way back."

She shrugged, feeling the rest of the magic float away on the breeze. "I was tired."

Colin eyed her, looking hurt and dispirited. "That's not it. You just didn't want to be seen with me."

Though it was the truth, Abby didn't want him to think that. As afraid as she was that he'd wound her heart, she also didn't want to cause him any pain, either. They'd both been hurt enough. It made her sad that she wasn't the girl who once would have been thrilled to have everyone in town know he'd asked her anywhere with him. And it made her feel small and mean to witness his pain.

"It isn't that I don't *want* to be seen with you." She reached out for him instinctively but let her hand fall without touching him. She wanted, needed, to convince him, but she couldn't risk that touch. She could explain, though. "It's that I *can't*. It isn't about you. It's about me. About them. And the mayoral race. Most voters wouldn't understand that you're not a conflict of interest for me. They'd ask what's going on and I'm not in the mood for a lot of questions or people misunderstanding what our being together means."

He moved closer, and her traitorous heart took off at a gallop. "What *does* it mean, Ab?" he whispered. His breath on her shoulder raised goose bumps on her arms in spite of the heat. He put his arm around her shoulder and tipped her chin up. And at his touch the magic of the night flooded her once again. Then he stroked his thumb across her lips. Abby didn't think she'd felt anything so blatantly erotic since that night so long ago when his lips had first met hers. The full moon let her see a sudden flare in his eyes and Abby knew he could tell exactly what he'd done to her.

"Colin, please," she protested, feeling her control slipping away. She needed to push him away.

He grinned. "I thought you'd never ask. I've been wanting to do this all night."

Then his lips silenced any protest she might have made.

His fingers trailed down her neck, to the valley between her breasts. He deepened the kiss and cupped first one breast then the other, sending need and hunger spiraling through her.

Abby found herself suddenly and entirely disconnected with life as she'd known it, as she'd lived it. Her nipples pebbled in response to his attention and a gnawing hunger invaded her center. Sensations she hadn't felt in years burned through her.

And just that fast she finally understood why she'd been unable to really respond to any other man since that fateful night.

She'd only ever wanted *him*.

It wasn't the night, or the moonlight that caused her enchantment. It was Colin.

She reached out, searching for something to hold on to, something to ground her, but she found the hard wall of his chest instead. Colin made a strangled sound and all she cared about was making him feel half of the pleasure he'd already given her.

Between that breath and the next, Abby found herself lying back on the blanket, cushioned by the thick grass beneath. Then Colin settled next to her, staring silently down at her. She opened her mouth, wanting to say something—anything—but he silenced her with his fingertip. "Shh," he whispered. And his face blotted out the moon as he braced himself over her on his forearms. When one of his legs settled between hers, she felt his thick arousal against her hip, felt him shudder at the contact.

The remembered thrill—the power she'd felt when she'd broken through his resistance that long-ago night—flooded her. Knowing that she could do that to him made her own desire blaze out of control just as it had the first time. She wanted—no, needed—to touch him. To feel his skin next to hers.

Colin must have had the same thought, because cool air flowed across her chest as the last button of her top gave way to his nimble fingers. His lips dusted kisses across her collarbone, filling her with a need so raw and gripping it took her breath. She reached to pull his shirt free of his slacks but her fingers were clumsy, her hands weak. She wanted to scream in frustration. She'd been dying to get her hands on his hot, muscled torso since the night he'd arrived…

Then his cell phone vibrated beneath her hand. Colin groaned and rolled away, reaching for the phone. Abby lay stunned. She was so lost in a fog of need and desire that she couldn't catch hold of her whirling thoughts to make sense of anything.

"Jess woke up," Colin said into the stillness, snapping his phone shut. "I have to go back. Come to my room, Ab. This isn't the place for this anyway. Come be with me."

His invitation was so close to the one he'd murmured that night when they'd both surrendered to the lure of desire that it felt as if she'd been dunked into an ice bath. She rolled away and scrambled to her feet. Staggering backward, she could only stare, her breathing harsh and uneven in her ears.

Longing for what she now knew she could only find in Colin's arms destroyed her ability to hide her feelings. Tears welled up in Abby's eyes as the pain of her self-imposed isolation crushed her.

But he could hurt you so much worse. Again.

What had she almost done? Was she out of her mind?

Colin was taken completely by surprise when Abby wrenched herself out of his arms. He reached out to steady her, but she nearly fell trying to evade him.

"No. No. Don't touch me," she sobbed as two fat tears fell from her widened eyes. "Please. I can't do this. You have to stop this."

"What? Trying to show you how I feel?"

"You're tearing me apart. I can't go to your room. Have you thought about Jessie? Suppose she woke up again and walked in."

He hadn't thought about that and it was completely out of character for him. Jess had never found him with anyone, but he didn't want to take a chance. "I can't go to your room, Ab. I have to be close in case she wakes up. She rarely does, but she just did and—"

"I'm not suggesting that! I'm saying we can't do this. At all. Ever."

"Why?" he demanded. His brain didn't seem to be working too well. Of course she hadn't been inviting him to her room. He raked a hand through his hair. "You felt what I felt. I know you did. Don't deny it."

"What did I feel?" She shook her head. "I don't know. How can I? How can you? I don't trust this. I can't."

"You got that in your head because you thought I'd used you. But now you know I didn't."

"Can you deny that you regretted what happened that night? That you panicked when you thought there might be a baby? I still remember you telling me not to thank you and tearing out of the room to talk to Harley. You could just as easily have flipped the lock on and waited for him to leave. But instead you ran. Didn't you?"

He couldn't even deny it. Dammit, he couldn't.

"And you wonder why I don't trust this? Because passion clouds my judgment. It probably clouds everyone's judgment and then they wake up married to the wrong person for the wrong reason and then they wind up in divorce court."

He saw it then. "This is about a lot more than us."

Abbey laughed bitterly. "Give the man a gold star. Of course it's about more than the mistakes of one night."

"It's your parents, too. I'm nothing like your father."

"Do you think my mother would have married him if my father had seemed to be the kind of person he turned out to be? And neither did—" She took a hitching breath then begged, "Please, just leave me alone."

But he couldn't. It was clear to him that he wasn't just falling in love with her. He'd always loved her. All he'd needed was to learn the truth, and years of anger had melted away, leaving only the total and helpless emotions he'd felt for her years before it was acceptable.

He sighed and stood, grabbing up the blanket. "I hear you, Abby—but I won't leave you alone. I can't." But she had raised some questions that haunted him. He raked a hand through his hair. "I'll see you in the morning."

"Not if I see you first. Good night, Colin," she said with an edge of desperation in her voice, and was gone, running across the meadow, away from Cliff Walk.

Though he hated to admit it, Abby had a point about impulsiveness and passion. Look at the mess thinking only about sex with Angelina had made of his life.

She'd been gorgeous and just enough older than he was to be mysterious. She was sophisticated and cultured and much sought after. Experienced. Just looking at her had made him burn with desire. It wasn't until she'd learned she was pregnant that his head had cleared enough to see her for the ambitious, shallow person she truly was.

Colin wouldn't give up Jessie for anything. Keeping her, raising her, had given him tremendous rewards, but there had been days when it had felt nearly impossible to go on. She'd had a lot of trouble teething and he'd still needed to show up on a job site at seven after spending the night walking her. One of those days he'd been so tired that he'd blown a nail right through his hand.

And there'd been the girl who'd robbed him while he slept, while he was in the army. After that, of course, there'd been Abby and her father's threat to destroy his parents. "Learn to keep your pants zipped, boy," his father had said as he'd walked Colin to the car that morning. He hadn't listened with Angelina. Didn't want to listen with Abby now. But maybe he'd better.

It wasn't that he doubted his feelings for her. This kind of all-encompassing need had to mean more than chemistry. He didn't just want Abby in bed. He wanted her at his side—forever.

Unfortunately, Abby doubted her feelings for him. So then how was he supposed to convince her they were meant for each other?

Showing her she could trust him would be a good

start, he guessed. After that, who knew? What he did know was that he'd do whatever it took. He put his hand to his chest and looked up at her darkened tower room.

The alternative didn't bear thinking about.

Chapter Eleven

Abby stood on the street outside Seek and Find Antiques and Collectibles, her unofficial campaign headquarters.

She stared at Muriel Haversham while the gray-haired proprietor of the oldest antique shop in town rattled on.

"I just need to hear you say you're still on our side, dear. This is so important to me. My father opened this shop in the twenties. If the river's going to take it, I'd rather just close my doors, sell the place and move into that new retirement village over near Moorestown. I was sure when Henry Chaffee said his son saw you with Colin McCarthy and his daughter at his farm, that your visit had something to do with you trying to convince that young man to change his mind about all the building out there. But then Francy and Ed swear they saw you at the movies with them. That sounded very much like a date. I'm sure no one will blame you. Colin is very handsome, dear. If you two are an item, you just tell me and we'll spin it."

"I'm hurt," Abby said, her heart pounding. Truthfully, she was devastated. People were speculating about her personal life—and questioning her ethics. "How could you think I'd turn my back on our cause for a man? I have tried every way I know how to talk Colin out of this." And she had.

She swallowed hard and continued. "Jessie doesn't know anyone here and she's lonely. I'm trying to fill in a little." A half-truth but still a truth.

Muriel wrung her hands. Seeing her so upset made Abby feel even more guilty. "But how can you deal with young Colin when you're on opposite sides of this issue?"

"Colin and I have agreed to disagree." That was true. "Look," Abby went on, reaching for more to say that would calm the woman down. Besides, what she told Muriel, the rest of the chamber of commerce would hear, as well. "Colin McCarthy was my best friend's big brother." Still truthful—sort of. "He was like…like my brother, too." Okay, now she was really stretching the truth. "Would you expect me to ignore my brother and niece because we disagreed about local politics?"

"So there's no truth to this at all?" Muriel asked.

Abby could hardly remember not loving Colin and the feelings were back. "I'm still opposed to his plans and to Harley. I'll fight with everything in me to stop them if elected. Tell anyone who's wondering about that. Tell everyone who'll listen. I'm counting on you."

"And we're counting on you, too."

She took Muriel's fine-boned hand. "I will stop this, but I probably have to get elected to do it. I won't let Colin get in the way. I promise."

She wouldn't. She'd avoid him just the way she'd warned him she would. What would she have done if anyone had seen them in that meadow? There'd have been no way to deny personal involvement.

As of now, it went no further. Could go no further. There'd be no repeat of last night.

Colin held open the swinging door between the dining room and kitchen and stuck his head in. "Genevieve, have you seen Abby and Jessie?"

"Do you really want to know?"

Now there was a confusing answer. "Why would you ask that?" he said, stepping in and letting the door swing shut behind him.

"Let's see," Genevieve said, then crossed her arms and leaned back against the kitchen's large center island. "She and Jessie finished putting the towels into the rooms that Abby cleaned this afternoon. And Abby did her office work while Jessie and I made cookies. She also said something about taking some brochures over to Juliana's office. She might be done with that by now and on to another *menial* job."

Well, that last phrase said it all. Even after a week and a half he knew exactly what Abby had done to rob him of his romance ally. "Ab told you she thinks I'm some kind of snob."

Genevieve glared then turned her back on him and banged pots around, a whole lot louder than he thought was necessary. Into the cacophony, she said, "She mentioned it. Now, if you'll excuse me, the hired help has dishes to do."

"Oh, for the love of God," he muttered, and charged across the room to the sink, grabbed a soup pot and some steel wool then proceeded to scrub it till it glistened. He realized when he shut off the sprayer that utter silence had fallen on the room. He turned and saw Genevieve staring at him wide-eyed.

"Well, what has your shorts in a knot now?" he demanded. "Am I not enough of a snob or what?"

She pointed to a stool. "Sit and talk. Because God knows I won't get the truth out of Abigail Hopewell. That girl could give a clam a lesson when she doesn't want to open her mouth. Which, I might add, never happened between us until you came along." Genevieve got a knife and began chopping onions. Then she looked up at him again, put down the knife and leaned on the island.

"I asked why she was avoiding you since the night you two took Jessie to the movies. She said it was because you were a snob about the work she does here, which didn't make much sense. I've seen you come back pretty filthy from that farm over there, but it isn't like Abby to lie, either. I've been had, haven't I?"

He'd thought he and Abby had talked this out, but maybe he'd been wrong. "Maybe she's right. It's not that I find work in any way, shape or form demeaning. It's Abby. I hate to see her doing work she was never meant to have to do. This shouldn't have happened to her. Or her sisters. Or her mother. I'm probably not saying this right…"

"You're in love with her."

Genevieve's simple statement stopped him in his tracks. He swallowed. He hadn't admitted it aloud, but he'd said it enough to himself that he was comfortable admitting it. He didn't think Abby was ready to hear it, but that didn't mean it wasn't true. "I'm in love with her," he admitted, then shook his head. "But Abby doesn't trust love. Or maybe she doesn't trust herself to recognize it. That's really why she's making sure we're never alone together. And she's made herself emotionally unavailable, which is worse. She won't even try to build a relationship." He plunked down on the bar stool at the center island. "I don't know what to do."

Hand propped on her ample hip, Genevieve looked at him as if he was slow-witted. "Woo her, you idiot. Find the one thing you can give her that no one else can, then show her how you feel. Wear her down! Now go find her and get to work." She wagged her finger at him, but he could tell she was fighting a smile. "And you better name your firstborn after me."

Colin stood and grinned, feeling better for the first time since Abby had fled from him in the meadow a week ago. "Okay," he agreed as he pushed open the door to Cliff Walk's formal Victorian dining room. "But I warn you," he tossed over his shoulder, "I intend to tell our son it's all your fault."

Genevieve roared with laughter. Colin wished he could hear Abby laugh again. He needed to get her to relax around him again. Her polite conversation and amused little chuckles were driving him nuts! He missed the Abby of the picnic and the movies and talking over ice cream in the kitchen with Jess. That was the old Abby, the girl it seemed he'd loved forever.

When he saw her amongst the vines with Jessie at her side talking to Samantha, Genevieve's words replayed themselves, *Find the one thing you can give her that no one else can.*

Maybe he could give her back some of the good memories of the times she'd had at Torthúil by showing her the progress he'd made. He knew seeing it in such a state of disrepair had bothered her. But she had promised to help with Jessie's room. Maybe he could use that as an excuse to get her there. It was the only thing he could think to do.

A niggling little voice that sounded an awful lot like his father whispered, *There's one other thing you could do. You could change your plans for Torthúil.* He sighed and sat behind the wheel of his pickup, watching his daughter and the woman he wanted for her mother almost as much as he wanted her for himself.

But he didn't think he could give up his dream.

He'd finished the drawings of the development. It would be so beautiful. The houses were top-of-the-line but smaller than the McMansions he'd seen going up all over the Philadelphia suburbs. He'd come up with over twenty styles that were united by the Pennsylvania fieldstone he planned to use in unique ways to personalize each one.

Maybe he could show her the renderings. Maybe her reaction wouldn't be as bad as he feared. But he was pretty sure it would be.

Colin shook his head and got out of the truck. He'd parked at the end of the lot for Bella Villa. Abby's serene gestures told him that she hadn't seen him or his truck. He purposely kept the tall, heavily laden vines between them. Thanks in part to the mesh Samantha had used to cover the vines, he was almost on top of the threesome when Jessie shouted his name and ran to him.

"Kitten! Did you have fun helping Abby today?" he called out as he scooped Jessie up into his arms and lifted her high in the air. Then, after settling Jess on his hip, he nodded to the two women.

"How's it coming over at your house?" Samantha asked.

Thank you for the opening, Samantha! Colin thought. "Actually, Sheetrock was put up in Jessi's room today and I finished refurbishing the windows in there, too. I got showered and dressed early to see if Abby would come over and help Jess pick colors. We could be back by dinner," he added, hoping to short-circuit any objections.

"Can you come, Abby? Can you?" Jessie pleaded, leaning out of Colin's arms toward Abby. "You promised to help Daddy make my princess room."

Samantha checked her watch. "Oops, look at the time. I need to get home to feed Nikki." She looked at Abby. "I just wanted to make sure you won't cave in if Mama gets really angry over us voting to keep Will on. We have to stick together. It's for her own good. She has to deal with Will and her feelings for him."

Abby let out an annoyed little humph. "I said I'll vote with you and I will. This had just better not backfire."

"Okay then," Sam said jauntily. "You kids have a nice rest of the day." Then she turned and sauntered toward her pickup parked on the access road on the other side of the field.

Abby opened her mouth and shut it while shooting daggers at him from those brilliant green eyes of hers. Then she seemed to realize she'd let her emotions show and regained her control.

But he'd seen. Anger was better than blankness, wasn't it? Better, but not what he wanted to deal with. Maybe he could distract her from their problems with this business Sam had been talking about!

"Can you tell me what that was all about, or was that cryptic bit of sister talk top secret?"

"Mama." Abby shrugged. "Will Reiger claims he's crazy about her. He's been here over six years, apparently trying to win her heart by helping her get the winery up and running. But he lied about being wealthy and pretended to be just a vintner. He was really a part owner of the winery where they met. Mama has this hang-up about wealthy men, thanks to my father. She doesn't trust them, or Will, now that she knows he lied.

"We outvoted her at a meeting earlier today and kept Will on instead of terminating his contract the way she requested. If you see fireworks going off over the office in the morning, you'll know he's told Mama we renewed his contract."

Colin whistled. "Your sisters think she's in love with him, I take it."

"Yep."

"And they think it's worth those fireworks, but you're not convinced."

Again she shrugged, looking thoughtful and sad. Then Jessie dragged his attention away from Abby. "Dad, you weren't apposed to put rocks on my walls. I wanted blue walls like in my tower room. Princesses don't have rocky walls."

"I think your daddy was talking about plaster that comes in sheets," Abby said, smiling at Jessie. But he still felt her tension and her sadness.

Jess giggled. "I know. I made a joke." She laughed again and fell sideways in his arms, trusting him to catch her, which of course he did. If only Abby would give him half that amount of trust.

"I seen Sheetrock all my life," Jess went on after he

got her stabilized on his hip again. "I sometimes get to write on extra pieces with my sidewalk chalk. It was a joke, right, Daddy?"

He nodded, his eyes still trained on Abby as she chuckled at Jess. It was pretty pathetic to be jealous of his kid, but at that moment he realized he'd give just about anything for Abby to look at him with that same helpless look of love in her eyes.

"My truck's right there. Come on. I really want to show you the progress I'm making at the house."

Abby stiffened. She didn't want to set foot in that house again. Especially not after the damage control she'd had to do after the last time. And she especially didn't want to go to the house with Colin. Besides the danger of being with him, that house held too many haunting memories.

But she'd made a promise to Jessie. "The first thing you need to do is pick out the fabric for the draperies and the cornice over the headboard. It's easier to match paint to the material than the other way around. Jess and I can go tomorrow, buy the material and I'll get you the right paint chip."

Abby saw a change in Colin's body language and expression. He didn't look annoyed but hurt. She felt small and mean to shun his company because their friendship might damage her chances in the election.

Avoiding being alone with him had seemed like a good way to protect both her heart and her campaign, but she had to admit it wasn't working on the personal front. She still cast him in her dreams every night. Sometimes in passion. Sometimes as the father of his adorable child. The last dream she'd had it had been in loss.

That one was new and had been the worst. She'd awakened in tears just that morning. He'd come to her in her dream to say he was giving up on her and Torthúil. He was going home—back to L.A.—but he hadn't wanted to disappear on her the way he'd been forced to before.

She should have been elated. There would be no added strain on the river from the Torthúil project. No more fear of heartbreak.

Until that morning, if she'd been asked by anyone, she would have said him leaving was exactly what she wanted. She would have said it was Jessie she would miss.

She could hide the truth from the world but not from herself.

Abby faced the truth. She didn't need a psychology degree to understand why it was nothing but Colin that mattered. It was clear that, no matter what she did, she couldn't get him out of her head.

Abby sighed. Maybe there was something to the old axiom that familiarity bred contempt. She'd tried everything else.

"Or instead of Jessie and I going it alone, we could all go to the mall now," she said, making a show of checking her watch. It was a good distance from town. Farther than the movies had been.

"Please, Daddy."

"Okay, but it's pretty far," he said, hesitant suddenly. "We'll never get there and back by six."

"No, but there's a food court," Abby said. "We ought to be able to find something relatively healthy for dinner there." She looked over at Jessie, whose elation had gone a little flat at the word *healthy* so she added, "And a certain someone can get a Happy Meal."

Colin grinned and added, "And play on the big tube slide and jump around in the balls with the other kids."

"Yea!" Jessie shouted, and nodded vigorously.

"Well, then, let's load up. We've got plans," Colin said, swinging Jessie around then wrapping her in a bear hug.

Abby stared at his muscular arms and chest outlined by his navy polo shirt. A sensual shiver raced through her as he set his child carefully on his shoulders. He was such a fascinating combination of gentleness and strength. Then she remembered how differently those hands had touched her in the meadow. How exciting they'd been in concert with his oh-so-talented mouth.

"Aren't you coming?" Colin called from about ten yards away.

Abby blinked. "Yes. Yes, of course," she said, but her suddenly dry throat made her answer sound more like a croak.

Where had her mind gone? Oh. Right. She'd been lost in utterly arousing sights and memories. Not a good idea.

Not good at all.

* * *

Two hours later they'd picked out bedding, draperies and big-girl furniture for Jessie's room. And the prettiest baby doll Abby had seen, except maybe her own long-lost childhood favorite.

Right at that moment, though, as Jessie ran full tilt up the ramp into the food-court play area, she reminded Abby more of Sammie than herself—all tomboy except for the doll under her arm. Jessie dove off the top of the ramp into a huge vat of plastic balls just as Abby and Colin settled on one of the benches at the gated entrance to the indoor playground.

"Jess really had a great time," Colin said, then turned to look at Abby. "I've had a great time, too, Ab. This meant a lot. Please stop shutting me out. We could be so good together if you'd only give us a chance."

"I'm not—"

"And please don't lie. Not to me and certainly not to yourself." He took her hand, glanced away to check on Jessie, then brought that sky-blue gaze back to her. He squeezed her hand then rubbed his callused thumb over the back of it.

Abby fought to ignore the surge of electricity that rushed up her arm to her breasts, which tightened in response. Luckily, except for darting glances toward the play area, he kept his eyes on her face.

"Look, I know you're afraid," he went on. "I get that. I know you don't trust yourself about this. I sure as hell know you don't trust me. But what do you really have to lose? I don't know for sure about how this last week has felt to you, but I know how it's felt for me. It sucked. It hurts like hell to feel like I'm on the outside of your life looking in."

"I'm not trying to hurt you. I'm just trying to—"

"To protect yourself," he finished before she could.

She blinked. "Will you stop finishing my sentences?" she demanded.

He grinned, though it was tinged with a sad sort of irony. "But I didn't get it wrong, did I?"

"No," she admitted.

"That's because we have so much history. So many feelings in common. Ab, trying to ignore what we feel in each other's arms…hell…within sight of each other is…well…it's just impossible. But you don't trust that. I get that, too. To tell you the truth, after the other night, I thought about what you'd said. Why you feel the way you do. The truth is, surrendering to passion has messed my life up even more than it has yours. Maybe I need to be just as wary as you are. Maybe I need to examine my feelings in another way."

Abby was surprised. "What? That isn't something I thought you'd say. And I guess that proves my point. I don't know you as well as you seem to think I do."

He nodded. "And you never will if the sum total of our conversations are what Jessie and you did today and idle chatter about the featured stories and weather forecast on the six-o'clock news. I'm not asking you to go to bed with me until we're both sure of our feelings."

She was about to respond when Jessie called out,

"Daddy, watch me." And then she pushed herself over the crest at the top of the slide to slip down the twists and turns of the shoot to the ground, shrieking with excitement all the way. And holding her doll in her lap.

An older woman sitting on another bench chuckled. "Isn't that just like a child? You wash and iron her clothes, curl her hair, dress her up and it's daddy she calls out to."

Abby was about to deny Jessie was hers when she once again saw what life as a family could be like. Instead of denial, she simply replied with the truth. "But he's such a wonderful father. No little girl ever had a better one."

"Then I'd say you're both blessed," the stranger said, and gathered up her knitting as two children around Jessie's age came barreling out of the gate shouting to their grandmother that they were starving.

"I'd be good to you, too, Ab," Colin whispered, his eyes pools of an emotion she was afraid to try translating into actual words. "Come on. Give us a chance."

She could only find the courage to nod, but then she found her voice. "How has passion messed up your life? Besides your mistake with me."

Colin raked a hand through his hair, looking a little self-conscious. "My relationship with Jess's mother was based on physical attraction, pure and simple."

He sat forward a little, leaning his elbows on his knees and hunching his shoulders, and stared at the ground between his feet. "It turned into a disaster. She wasn't getting anywhere in L.A. and had planned to head back to Brazil where she'd been a minor star. But then she found out she was pregnant. Her parents were wealthy and she was raised in convent schools. I think she hit the States and went a little wild. I know all about being raised Catholic. That guilt mentality was in there somewhere and I used it to talk her into agreeing to have the baby. She married me only so I'd pay the bills. We never lived together as a married couple. We had a prenup. I wasn't that dumb. I got sole custody of Jessie from day one. She hung around for nearly a year, collecting alimony and waiting for an annulment she applied for with the church. During that time, she saw Jess on occasion, but she was never a real mother. Once she got back in shape and had her annulment, she breezed out of our lives never to return."

Abby thought back to those early days for Caro when she'd taken on Jamie. How hard it had been for her sister to pick up the pieces of her life and raise the child they'd all thought was their half brother. And they had all chipped in as much as possible. Suppose Caro had been alone? Suppose Jamie had been a newborn?

Abby focused on Colin, who was watching Jessie. He wore that openly loving smile he usually did when he had his daughter in his sight. Abby had to wonder where she'd ever find a man more worthy of a second chance.

Chapter Twelve

Colin zipped his jeans, tossed the towel over his shoulder and walked into Jessie's princess room at Cliff Walk. He looked around and ruefully shook his head. He hated to admit it, but he kind of liked the girly decor. Maybe because it reminded him of Abby. It was elegant and feminine, but there was strength and boldness in the design.

Just like Abby.

She'd gone out on a limb with the scale of the ornate gold cornice that hung over the bed just the way she taken a bold chance by standing up to Harley Bryant. Though Colin still didn't agree with her position on his plans, he applauded the way she fought for her cause.

Now if she'd just come to a place where she could

be equally brave in her personal life. It had only been two days since Abby promised to give them a chance to get to know each other. They'd tried to have dinner alone on the terrace the night before, but rain had caused them to move it to tonight. They'd all eaten in the kitchen with Genevieve, instead. But with Jess and the cook there, private discussion was impossible. The other Cliff Walk guests had gathered in the parlor after dinner so they'd had no place to be alone. He'd needed to work on his drawing of Torthúil Gardens for a meeting with a bank earlier today, so he hadn't been able to invite her to spend time with him in his room after Jessie's bedtime.

The sound of Jessie chatting to her baby doll about the day's activities drew his attention. Abby had unearthed an antique cradle and a less valuable high chair from her own childhood for Jess to play with. They were arranged in the corner next to Jess, who sat in her little rocking chair from their house in L.A. She cradled her baby doll in her arms carrying on an interesting one-way conversation about grapes and how they grew.

If the amount of dirt his daughter wore was any indication, she was having a blast at the kids' camp with Samantha and Nic. "Your turn in the bathtub, kitten," he told her.

"Abby promised to come help," she said. "We should wait. I don't want to dis-da-point her." She gave the chair another determined push.

"Abby had a lot of new people arrive today. Another couple came just as I got back here. She's probably tired. Let's give her a break, okay? Somehow I think she'll live through her disappointment if you're already clean when she can make time to come up here."

Jessie stared at him, looking a bit indignant. "Abby promised, Daddy, and she always keeps her promises," she told him, sounding just a bit more grown-up than he'd been prepared for.

Jessie went back to her baby doll and he took a second to decide if this was one of those times he should insist they do things his way.

A knock at the door got him off that particular disciplinary hook and attested to the fact that Abby did indeed keep her word to Jessie. He could only hope she was as faithful to her promise to him.

Jess danced over to the door and threw it open before he'd gathered his wits enough to even move.

"I have extra fluffy towels for the princess of the tower," Abby called out as she came in.

He walked forward, kissed her on the cheek and took the linens from her.

"Escuse me, Daddy," Jess said, planting her hands on her hips. "Abby came to see me. We were gonna have a bath now that I put baby Mary Beth to bed."

"Well, I can see I'm not wanted here," he said, pretending to pout. "I'll see you both in a few minutes. Try to stay dry, Ab."

"Jessie should be the only one getting wet," Abby told him confidently as she shifted her attention to Jessie. "And of course, a lady's bubble bath takes a bit longer than a shower so we'll be a while."

"A bubble bath!" Jess squealed.

Colin held up his hands. "I'll just go to work on some drawings in my room. Have fun, ladies," he told them then beat a hasty retreat. He was tempted to disabuse Abby of her plan to stay dry. Jessie was not a docile bather. She liked to splash and make waves in the tub. Every time he'd tried to use girly soaps on Jessie, he'd wound up smelling like flowers, then had to take all manner of abuse from his friends.

Colin pulled his drawing board out of the corner of the sitting room and set it up in front of the windows to take advantage of the waning sunlight. After he'd finished dressing, he got down to work. He was nearly done with the blueprints of the entire project, but today he really wanted to work on the presentation for the zoning board. For ten minutes he worked on adding a few more landscaping elements to his rendering of Torthúil Gardens. In the background, giggles and outright roaring laughter leaked through the bathroom door. It was music to his ears. He glanced down at the floor by the door and grinned. Laughter wasn't the only thing leaking through the door.

About to grab his towel to stanch the flood and save the hardwood floors, he was interrupted by the ringing of his cell phone.

"Hello," he said, flipping the little phone open as he snatched up the towel and dropped it onto the floor by the door, toeing it against the bathroom's marble threshold to sop up his side of the flood.

"Yo," a stranger's voice said with a slight echo.

"This is the O'Donnell Quarry truck. I've got a load of fieldstone to deliver, but I can't find your driveway."

He'd given up on the delivery when four-thirty came and went. But he'd forgotten that Torthúil's mailbox had blown down in last night's rainstorm. No wonder the guy couldn't find it. He tried giving the location by using the entrance to the Hopewell property as a marker, but the driver wasn't too thrilled.

"Buddy, I've driven up and down River Road five times and I'm sick of lookin' at it. I'm headed back out from Hopetown again now. I'm about two miles outside town. Would you mind just coming out to the road and flagging me down? This is my last delivery and my family's waiting on me for dinner."

Colin sighed. So much for drawing. "Be right there. Why don't you slow down so you don't pass us again. I'll be there in a few minutes. My truck is black." He even gave the guy the make and model just to be safe, since Sam's husband, Nic, drove a black truck, too. The way his day had gone, Nic would be sitting at the end of the manor's driveway ready to turn onto the road at a crucial moment. He didn't need his fieldstone mixed in with the retaining wall Nic was having built at the manor to bolster their flood protection.

He cast one last look at the drawing on his work-table and went to ask Abby to look after Jess while he was gone. He pushed open the door and promptly forgot to breathe. Abby sat with her eyes closed in what looked like a yoga position. Her long legs were folded up like a pretzel under her flowing pink flowered skirt. Her back was poker straight and her arms were behind her back. Her breasts were barely obscured by her pastel-pink, soaking-wet T-shirt and bra. Jess, covered in bubbles was trying to mirror the position.

"Ab," he began, but his voice came out in such a low register he barely recognized it. Abby's eyes flew open, but his own eyes betrayed him by casting themselves back to the most interesting part of the bathroom's current scenery.

Her beautiful, perfect breasts peaked as the air from his room touched her.

"Oh," she cried after a long silent beat and grabbed a towel to hug against herself.

With the scenery made so much less interesting, Colin managed to focus on Abby's adorably pink face. He grinned. "Last I heard you weren't going to be the one taking the bath?"

"What do you want?" she demanded, not meeting his gaze.

"Daddy. Get out. I told you this is 'upposed to be girl time," Jess scolded.

"Yeah, Daddy," Abby chimed in, using a childlike voice, her sense of humor obviously recovered.

"I have to run back over to Torthúil. The quarry's driver is trying to deliver the rock we picked out for the fascia on the farmhouse's addition. The guy can't find the driveway so I'm going over to flag him down. It shouldn't take long, but could you keep an eye on Jess."

"Take my magic rock so you know if it's the right color."

He'd carried that rock for nine years. He knew the color. "Go," Abby said, understanding in her eyes. "We're fine right here. I'll meet you on the terrace for dinner."

"Thanks. Don't worry, kitten. I know the color. You be good for Abby," he ordered, and started to back out and shut the door, but he couldn't resist teasing Abby. He'd never been able to resist it. He tucked his head back in. "By the way. Nice....T-shirt," he quipped, and pulled the door shut again.

Half a second later, he heard the soft sound of the towel hitting the door as he sauntered out of his room, laughing.

Abby had delivered Jessie to Genevieve, and the child was now ensconced at the island in the kitchen helping Cliff Walk's amiable chef finish up preparations for the guests' dessert. After that, the two of them had plans for their own "special" dinner.

Looking at herself in the hall mirror, Abby turned, admiring the back of her newest sundress. This one was Colin's idea. He'd insisted on buying it as a thank-you for taking care of Jessie.

She'd tried to resist. She'd even resisted when Jessie added her own brand of prodding to the mix. But she'd given in and tried it on when Colin threatened to resort to Jessie's tactics. Since that included jumping up and down shouting, "Please, please, please," Abby had laughingly given in. But she'd also warned him that the next time she'd actually hold out just to see him perform Jessie's begging dance in public.

Now, on her way down to meet Colin on the terrace, she had to stop at their suite because Jessie had forgotten her doll when she'd gone down to dinner. He'd mentioned wanting to take Jessie for a walk later and she wanted to take her doll along. Abby stopped at the linen closet on her way to the tower suite and grabbed the clean towels she needed to deliver there anyway. She'd used every last one in the bathroom to sop up the water and bubbles that had flooded the bathroom floor.

She unlocked the door and grabbed the baby doll under her arm, laughing again when she noticed Dog-dog tucked into the baby doll's cradle. Clearly the reigning favorite, Jessie's stuffed pal would never truly be replaced. As Abby hung the towels up in the bathroom, she noticed the air was still awfully moist. She opened the door to the sitting room hoping to dissipate more of the moisture.

Colin's drawing board sat in the middle of the room, beckoning to her. She walked hesitantly over to it, wondering about this talent she hadn't known he had when they were younger. And there, spread out for her examination, was the detailed rendering of Torthúil Gardens. With the knowledge she'd gained from the planning of the winery and the architect's rendering of the renovations on Cliff Walk she could read them easily.

If it was anywhere else, she would have loved everything about it. It looked like a sleepy village that had sprouted up out of the earth. It was an homage, in native Pennsylvania fieldstone, both to Colin's Irish and farming heritages. But the number of structures, the wide cement pathways and the many streets as well as the tennis courts and pool, were all made of nonpermeable surfaces and were going to create a great deal of runoff while stealing important drainage acres. This couldn't help but cause more trouble when the rain swelled the river. Would it add feet to the next flood? No. Inches? Probably. But how many times had the river come within inches of spilling over—within a foot of annihilating the town?

"I can see you don't appreciate my efforts," Colin said from the doorway.

Abby looked up. She'd been engrossed in her thoughts she hadn't heard the door open. He didn't look angry, but he wasn't happy, either.

"I'm sorry. It wasn't trying to spy. It was just sitting here. I put fresh towels in the bathroom and I opened the door to let the room air better and—"

"Abby," Colin cut in. "I don't mind that you saw them. I was going to show them to you when I finished a few more details. If I look less than thrilled, it's that I could see your opinion in your expression. Imagine someone telling you your baby is ugly."

Her heart ached. For him and her. "But it's not ugly. It's wonderful. Breathtaking really. But think of the runoff, Colin. It can't help but add to the problem and look at all the acres of impeded drainage there'll be."

Colin walked to the board and stared down at it. She saw his eyes traverse the entire drawing, stopping some places, skipping over others. "The courts could go to clay, but that's not much more permeable. I could maybe change some other materials but that's going to kill my bottom line." His frown deepened as he stared down at his beautiful work. "Maybe if I..."

She could almost feel his misery. If only he could let go of his need to build his net worth quickly. If her father had learned to mind his own business, Colin wouldn't be so driven today! She'd been eighteen.

"Colin, you are so incredibly talented. If Hopetown weren't threatened by every building erected, I'd be at your side pushing this through the zoning board, but I have to be true to my beliefs. Try to let go of your bottom line. No one but you cares how many zeros it takes to estimate your financial worth. Think about it." She patted his arm. "We agreed to disagree on this and not discuss it. But let me say this one last thing. Your dad would be so proud to see what you designed to honor his heritage. Now let's go have dinner and let's not talk about this anymore." He shot her a wry look. She sighed and squeezed his arm. "Okay, let's not talk about it anymore *tonight*."

Dinner awaited them when they went out to the terrace. As requested Genevieve had gone easy on the romance. Cold fried chicken, potato salad and shaved cucumbers and onions that had been soaked in oil and vinegar. Accompanied by a crisp green salad, it was the perfect cool meal for a steamy August evening.

After they ate they stopped by the kitchen and took Jessie for a long walk through the beautiful wildlife preserve Sam had designated for the benefit of Belle Villa and Cliff Walk guests. Abby was a little wary, knowing they'd wind up at the meadow where but for the phone call they'd probably have made love under the stars just a little over a week ago.

But they took a different, longer route, and as they walked along the finely ground mulch of the pathways, she realized the atmosphere was different. The sensual energy that always flowed between her and Colin was more muted with Jessie along. Each holding one of Jessie's hands, they wove their way across the plateau through the heavily forested land, then circled a meadow of purple clover before plunging back into the shadow of the trees.

Stone benches were scattered throughout the preserve at points of interest. Plaques along the pathways identified and explained the many local horticultural specimens and several sculptures by local artisans dotted the landscape.

When the trees gave way to the larger meadow she'd been leery of revisiting, a family of deer stood at its center grazing, dissipating the rest of her worry. At the beautiful sight, they all froze in place. Colin quickly squatted down next to Jessie, signaling for her to be quiet.

The air was still, but the big buck's head came up and he sniffed. They watched as, satisfied that his family was safe, he went back to grazing. Then a sweet spotted fawn drifted out of the cluster and Jessie's sharply indrawn breath must have alerted the buck. He broke the group and they all leaped into action, running off into the undergrowth.

"Why that baby had spots and not the mommy and daddy?"

Colin explained about nature's way of providing camouflage for the more helpless members of the animal kingdom. It gave Abby a chance to look down at them, their heads together, their features so alike and their coloring so different. Her heart never failed to soften at the look of utter devotion that came over Colin's handsome face when a special moment like this occurred between him and his child.

Abby's desire to be part of their little circle grew each day and she was beginning to feel that was happening. She did want that. She really did. If only she could be sure she wasn't being influenced by the kind of untrustworthy feelings Colin had always caused in her. She knew he thought modesty was the reason she'd grabbed the towel that afternoon, but that couldn't be further from the truth.

What had happened was that when she'd seen the desire in his burning blue gaze her entire body had tightened in needy response. Since her nipples had been the only telltale sign, she'd hidden them as quickly as she could. It had diverted his attention and for that she was thankful. She knew he'd only been teasing her but moments like that made her doubt the feelings she thought were growing between them.

Was there even a way to separate desire from affection and compatibility when there was so many nearly uncontrollable urges zinging back and forth between two people?

Chapter Thirteen

Abby drove up Torthúil's driveway three days after she'd seen Colin's drawings. He'd asked her to come over to see his progress on the house and help him figure out the right layout for Jessie's room. She'd been avoiding this, and the closer she got the more tension knotted her stomach.

She drove from under the tunnel of leaves and hit the brakes. Abby felt suddenly out of normal space and time. She could hardly believe her eyes. The progress made in the past two weeks was startling. There were workers everywhere. It scarcely looked like the dilapidated place she had seen on her prior visit.

Gone was the sagging porch. In its place was an exact replica of the original as it had been in better days. This porch, however, extended across the front of an addition that nearly doubled the length of the original house.

"Hey, Ab," Colin called, as he stepped out the door of the addition onto the new porch. He waved her forward toward a crude cracked-stone parking pad. Smiling broadly, he hurried toward her car along a temporary wood-plank walkway. He was clearly glad to see her.

When he pulled her car door open, a cacophony of sounds greeted her. There was the steady thwack of air hammers echoing from somewhere in the back, the high-pitched whir of power screwdrivers and the buzz of a circular saw. "There's an awful lot going on," she said as she accepted his hand to help her out of the low-slung car.

"Yeah, we're really making progress," he said, keeping her hand as she picked her way over the rough stones to the planking he'd traversed moments before. He walked backward up the plank ramp to steady her. She was grateful, looking down at the mud pit beneath the temporary ramp. As if on cue and just before they reached the porch, a rumble from above had him glancing up. It had rained hard last night, and another series of thunderstorms were bearing down on them.

"Is the weather holding you up?" she asked.

"We're just about under cover. The back roof on the addition should be buttoned up within the hour. I'm not used to rain holding me up unless it stops work entirely." He shrugged. "In L.A. it's either a deluge or sunny."

She could put this off—this day of confronting the ghosts of the past. She could blame the weather for her cowardice. “Maybe I should come back another day so you can finish the roof on time.”

Colin shook his head, dashing her hope of a reprieve. “I wasn’t working with the men up on the roof anyway. I’ve been refurbishing the windows and fabricating trim so the addition matches the old section. These guys never did any restoration work so I’m on my own with that stuff.”

Without a thought she reached up and brushed the sawdust off his shoulders. And felt a sensual jolt. Why did the most innocent of touches have to muddle her brain? “Are you going to change the focus of your work?” she asked, trying to distract herself—trying to think and not feel. Her feelings around him were tumultuous and unruly. How *did* anyone think when they felt like this? “You said you’d specialized in restoration in California, but now you’ll be doing mostly new construction.”

Their footsteps echoed on the new porch decking and the smell of freshly cut wood swirled in the air. He stopped, all his attention on her. “I built several custom homes back there, but I’d be lying if I said I don’t usually enjoy restoration the most.

“Still,” he said, and slapped his hand onto one of the new porch columns as he looked back at the old section of the house, “rebuilding this house and melding it with the addition is the most fun I’ve had in years.” His eyes took on a faraway look. “I used to lie on that old glider—you remember, the one that sat there under the living room widows. I'd think of all the things I'd do to the place if I had the money. It's what drew me to architecture in the first place."

"I'd wondered about that," she said, and grinned. "Remember that tacked-together tree house you handed off to Tracy for her birthday one year? I'm glad to see your design skills have improved."

"Hey, some of it was still up there when I got back. Before Jess got any ideas, I pulled it down. That thing was ugly as sin..." he said his voice trailed off. He was suddenly lost in thought. Then his gaze focused.

On her.

Sometimes he looked at her as if he was trying to see into her soul.

Sometimes she thought he could.

And it made her nervous. "So, back to the present day and your plans for your company," she said.

He blinked. "Right. Some of these guys seem interested in learning restoration and doing projects like this one and as I said, I'm loving it, so I'm guessing I'll work toward having two divisions."

Just being there was difficult enough. Before they strayed closer to uncomfortable topics like new buildings or their relationship, Abby suddenly wanted to get this tour of the house over with. "So show me what you've done with the old place."

"I guess you noticed I matched the clapboards on the new section of the porch to the old one. The rest of the addition above the porch roof, and both back and sides, will be faced with stone."

"The infamous fieldstone of the lost driver?"

He nodded. "It'll be on the whole porch apron, too, but..." He stopped, looking a little abashed. "I'm sorry, you probably couldn't care less about construction details."

"It sounds beautiful," she assured him.

He nodded again and stepped back, gesturing to the door. "So, ready for the tour?"

"As I'll ever be. Lead on."

He stepped over the threshold and she got her second surprise as she followed him inside. It was a big room with a beautiful large fieldstone fireplace that was nearly complete. "This will be a country kitchen," he told her. "I sort of see a big round table in front of the fireplace."

He wasn't kidding. It was completely open and took up what seemed to be the entire first floor of the addition. Abby noticed plumbing rough ins, under a wide window. Anyone standing at the sink would look out at the elm where they'd picnicked.

"I'm about to order the cabinets." He pointed to several samples that were mock-ups of actual cabinet fronts. "I like the painted ones and the cherry, but I can't decide which I like best."

The answer seemed obvious to Abby. "Why not use both? Use the painted ones for the cabinets. With the beadboard panel in the door they'd really punch up the country look this place calls for. I mean, it did start life as a farmhouse." She pointed to the square he'd taped in the middle of the room. "I assume that's supposed to be a center island."

He nodded but seemed a little tentative.

Abby went on anyway. He'd asked, after all. "Well, then you could use the cherry for the island. Make it look like a big piece of furniture. The room would take on a sort of casual elegance."

He tilted his head a little and smiled. "Just like you. Casually elegant. Maybe you could moonlight as my decorator."

She blushed at his appraisal and found herself not immediately rejecting his offer to work with him. She had plenty to do at Cliff Walk, but she loved decorating. And working with him would be fun since she loved…no… she didn't know if she loved Colin. How would she ever know if she couldn't figure out how to separate the sexual pull between them from deeper, more lasting feelings?

He was right. They'd only know by spending time together. Getting to know each other.

Abby determinedly put thoughts of the future away and followed Colin toward the back of the kitchen. That was when she realized the addition was L-shaped. Suddenly she got her bearings and it knocked the breath right out of her.

The next room would be the room that had been off the kitchen. The converted sleeping porch. His room. Somehow her hand wound up in his again and he pulled her forward.

When she had to step down, she realized what he'd done. He had torn it down and replaced it with a room that was light, airy and a completely different shape than the one that had been there before. Instead of a small square room this one was a long rectangle that extended the length of the original house with a high ceiling formed by a gabled roof.

Colin put his arm around her. His scent enveloped her, but this time instead of near raging desire, or fear of it, she felt cherished and safe. "I demolished my old room, sweetheart. This'll be the family room."

She noticed the beginnings of fieldstone going in on the end wall. "A fireplace in here, too?"

"Yep. It'll go right up to that engineered ridge beam. And there'll be one in the master, too, but it'll be less rustic with a traditional wooden mantel."

He led back up a step and into what had been the old kitchen, but it was unrecognizable as the site of the most humiliating moment of her life. Now it was just a square room covered with Sheetrock. She looked at Colin and understood. He'd done this and demolished his old room for her sake. She was nearly sure of it. He'd tried to wipe away the bad memories with his talent. He'd turned his childhood home backward…

For her.

"What will this room be?" she found the courage and voice to ask.

Colin relaxed. She understood at least part of the message he was trying to convey with the house. She still didn't know he had begun redesigning this home with her in mind. But, for today, what she had learned was enough.

He'd been tremendously relieved when she'd jumped in with her ideas on the cabinet selection. He couldn't be sure she'd wind up living there but he couldn't imagine them not remaining friends at least. He still hoped they'd be more but, if not, she could be comfortable visiting him and Jessie with the changes. How he'd ever cool his libido around her if it worked out that way was a worry, though.

He wanted her so damn bad.

He just had to convince her they belonged there together.

"I'm thinking I'll make this my office. I'll just hang my shingle out on River Road and be here for Jess. Want the upstairs tour?"

She smiled, looking excited now and not as if she expected to encounter a ghost lying in wait around the next corner. He tried to be content with that.

As he stepped into what had been the dining room, he explained that he planned to flip the living room and dining room to give the latter easier access to the kitchen. Then he showed her through the upstairs.

He tried not to picture her in the master suite, but that was impossible once she'd stepped inside. She walked to the French doors and he explained the wrought-iron balcony he had on order for outside the doors. He could picture them sitting out there having coffee at a little bistro table watching the sunrise.

Then thunder rumbled again. Louder. Closer. She stepped away from the windows as the sky opened up and rain poured down. "We'd better get going on the room. I want to be ready to go when this lets up," she said, turning toward him.

Colin nodded. He didn't trust his voice. He'd made his parents' room into Jessie's room. This way Abby wouldn't need to go into Tracy's room if she didn't want to. But, as if drawn there, or like an old, familiar habit, she opened Tracy's door and stood staring.

He hadn't touched it yet because by some miracle it was the only room not damaged by the leaking roof. And since the door had been closed since her death, nothing had been destroyed by the pests that had invaded the vacant house. All he'd done was toss out the musty mattress and box spring. Even Tracy's posters still hung where she'd left them—in the room Abby had help decorate for her birthday one year.

"It's a shrine," Abby said in a choked voice.

And Colin knew she was right. His parents hadn't moved a thing. It was the only room where furniture had been left behind. What on earth had they been thinking? Now he'd be the one who had to tear it apart.

Colin stepped in when Abby walked over to a Guns N' Roses poster. She turned back to him, a smile on her face and tears in her eyes. "Buns N' Noses," she sniffled. "Your dad used to tease her all the time calling them that. She loved Guns N' Roses."

She walked to a slightly yellowed poster of a castle. In front of it was a table full of dragon and fairy statues.

Abby reached out and trailed her finger across the wings of one of the larger dragons. "We should put these in Jessie's room. They'd go with the princess theme. Don't you think? Tracy wouldn't want a shrine, Colin. She'd want her niece to have these."

"You bought them for her, didn't you?"

In a soft, barely audible voice, she said, "Birthdays. Christmases. She loved fantasy. The more romantic the better." And a sob escaped her throat.

He was across the room in the next heartbeat, pulling her into his arms, holding her tight. He realized when a tear fell from his own eyes on the hand he'd burrowed in her hair that he was sharing his grief with her.

"Shh, sweetheart," he begged, hoping to offer comfort, trying to calm her and himself. But much as he hated seeing her cry, he knew this was right. They'd both finally grieved the only way they ever should have. Together. Because other than his parents, no one had loved his little sister more than he and Abby.

When he thought the most emotional moments had passed for both of them, and he had control of his voice, Colin took her by the shoulders and moved back a step. She looked up, eyes still full of tears, her nose adorably red. She pulled her lower lip under her top teeth, clearly reaching for composure.

"You were right," he told her. "She wouldn't want this abandoned shrine. She'd want everyone to go on living. She'd want Jess to have her fantasy collection. She'd want us together if that's what we decide we want."

Abby nodded.

"I knew my sister. Even though she was angry at you for what she thought had happened, I know she loved you. She wouldn't have been angry otherwise. And she would have wanted us to grieve together. So, now that we've done that, it's time to let her rest in peace."

Abby nodded again. Then, smiling bravely, she said, "Let's go plan Jessie's room." She looked back up at Tracy's castle poster. "I have an idea. How about I paint Jessie a mural? After all, what's a princess without a kingdom."

Colin thought of the other tower room at Cliff Walk and wondered if he'd finally rescued his adult princess from her enchanted tower.

Chapter Fourteen

Colin sat at the kitchen island eating a fast breakfast with Jess. He'd gotten back to Cliff Walk a little late last evening. After he'd walked Abby to her car, he'd gotten a call from the bank officer he'd spoken with during the previous week.

First Trust had picked up the financing. He'd met the bank president and signed the papers within hours. Then he'd stopped by to see Harley Bryant so he could tell him to kiss the project goodbye.

Harley had been furious. Apparently he'd forgotten his drunken confession at the bar and Colin's reaction to it. It had been a whole lot more satisfying to tell Harley off this time since he was sober. And the best part was that Colin had hit him where it really hurt—in his wallet.

He'd gone back to the house to check on the progress there and found that the guys working on the roof had gotten it finished before a whopper of a thunderstorm was supposed to hit. They'd left him a note saying they'd buttoned the place up good and tight before knocking off for the day. He'd checked things over just to make sure all the window and door openings were secured with scrap fiberboard and plenty of screws.

It had been seven by the time he'd gotten to Cliff Walk. He honestly didn't know what he'd have done without Abby taking care of Jessie this past month. He hoped he'd never have to find out.

Then, because he'd missed so much time with Jess, he'd spent the entire evening with her. He'd made it clear to Abby that she was welcome to join them, but she'd declined. He'd given up trying to convince her when he'd finally understood her reason.

She was still obsessed with protecting the sacred Hopewell name, having appointed herself the guardian of the family legacy. He hadn't rescued his princess at all.

Colin was sure her reluctance to spend even one second in the sitting room of the suite—especially in the evenings—was worry over possible gossip. He intended to pin her down after breakfast for a serious talk. He was pretty sick of being less important than a name.

Samantha's husband, Nic, appeared in the doorway with Jamie, Abby's nephew. "Have we any Kid

Campers here on this beautiful morning?" Nic called out in his distinctive continental cadence.

"Me," Jessie yelled back, sticking her hand in the air like a regular school kid.

"Well, then, if you have finished your breakfast, come along," Nic said.

"Okay," Jess answered, and turned in her chair to jump down.

Colin put his hand out to stop her forward motion. "Forget something?"

Jess rolled her eyes comically. "Sorry. Can I be escused?"

He fought a smile. "Of course, kitten. Don't forget your bag of extra clothes. It'll be pretty muddy out there today." She went to slide forward and he stopped her again. "What about my hug-kiss?"

She gave him a quick kiss and a cursory hug and said as fast as possible, "Hug-kiss." And then she wiggled down and was gone.

He watched her as she took Jamie's hand and skipped off.

"And before you know it, she'll be going off to the movies with some big strong male you want to strangle for even looking at your precious little girl," Juliana Hopewell warned from the kitchen doorway.

He sighed. "Does it ever get easier?"

"Easier? No. Different? Definitely." She walked in and sat across from him. "We spend our time watching them, hoping and praying they're happy. I, for instance, am seeing the most remarkable changes in Abby lately."

Colin sighed. "Sam already warned me not to hurt her."

Juliana smiled. "I'm here with a different kind of warning. I applaud the fact that you've shaken her life up a bit. It's wonderful to see her just brimming with emotion the way she used to be. But right now she's in her office and I think there may have been steam coming from her ears. I would tread carefully were I you, but I'd see if I could put out the fire—and quickly."

Colin nodded, tossed down his napkin and stood. "Thanks for the warning."

Juliana smiled and sailed back out the door.

Abby's office door was closed so he knocked. No sense teaching the kid manners if he forgot his own. Then the door swung open. Juliana was right.

Steam.

"Well, look who's here," Abby all but growled.

He pretended to look behind him. "Just me, not Jack the Ripper," he quipped, trying for a little levity to defuse what looked like a ticking time bomb. Was he the one who'd thought mad was better than no emotion just last week?

"How about Benedict Arnold?" she spat back.

Colin raised his eyebrows. "I would think to turn traitor I'd have to have planned it. I promise I'm as loyal as Jamie's dog."

She swung her arm inward toward the room in a grand gesture. "Well, come on in and I'll enlighten you!"

He was halfway across the room when the door

slammed shut behind him. Colin winced. He'd stirred her all right. She whizzed by him and plunked herself down in her desk chair.

He took his time as he walked forward, stopping to look over a bunch of campaign posters that sat in a box ready for distribution. Another held brochures about her platform. They were already addressed and post-marked. On the wall behind her head was a white board with statistics and a bar graph showing where she needed to do the most campaigning.

He sank as casually as he could into the chair on his side of the desk and suddenly felt like a kid called to the principal's office. He didn't much like the feeling, either. "So, what is it you think I've done?"

She grabbed up a newspaper and sent another glare at him. It was a copy of the morning edition of the *Bucks County Courier*.

"I was hoping to get their endorsement. I probably can kiss that opportunity goodbye. Let's see why," she said, obviously preparing to read. " 'What's going on up at Hopewell Winery? Specifically at Cliff Walk, the B and B located on the property? Cliff Walk is partially owned and operated by mayoral candidate Abigail Hopewell—a *supposed* proponent of zero tolerance for anything that includes impeded ground permeability.' It goes on to tell all about your project, who you are and what your credentials are."

"That isn't exactly news. The zoning meeting was nearly four weeks ago."

She looked up, glared at him and went back to

scanning the article for whatever else was in it that had lit her fire.

"'It has come to this reporter's attention that McCarthy and his young daughter have been residing at Cliff Walk, where Ms. Hopewell also lives full-time. Sources close to the pair tell us these two apparently have a past romantic history and have been seen out and about together, looking like much more than friends.'"

Colin sighed. "I thought we decided to explain that you aren't changing your opinion and plan to fight even though we've been friends for years."

"I tried to defuse the situation that way. That isn't why I'm so angry." She looked back at the offending article. "Ah, here it is. 'Mayor Bryant, who initially supported McCarthy's project has, on further consideration, instructed his bank to pull its funding and has withdrawn his support. Colin McCarthy has procured other financing.'

"'The question now is, has our local green candidate suddenly gone over to the dark side? Is she being swayed by an affair of the heart to abandon all those high-sounding pledges about conservative land use? It wouldn't be the first time a Hopewell abandoned principles for the opposite sex.'

"'What say you, Ms. Hopewell?'"

She slammed the paper down and Colin fought the urge to wince again at the fire in her eyes. "What *am* I supposed to say now, Colin? What?" she demanded.

He tried to stay calm. "How about you start with the

fact that Harley Bryant is a liar. I started looking for other financing when I found out what he'd done to us nine years ago."

"You could have warned me."

"I guess I forgot to mention it. At the time I was more occupied with coming to grips with all the lies and misunderstandings in our past. I only made it official with Harley yesterday. I have to say this for him, he works fast. I just managed to catch him as he left the bank at around five-thirty. I told him then that I was definitely pulling the project from Bryant Savings and Loan. He was pissed, but I didn't think even he would try to spin it this way."

She threw up her hands. "He's a practiced liar. It isn't news. Everyone should know it by now, but the paper still printed it."

"Had you considered handling it the way you'd planned? Tell the reporter that what you do in your personal life is none of her or anyone else's business. You could explain that you can keep an open mind because you're honest, unlike the current mayor, and you can tell her that I altered the plans to better fit with community needs. I cut the clubhouse because I didn't know Bella Villa even existed and—"

"That makes it look more than ever like I changed my position for personal gain. You eliminated the one thing that would have given us competition. If I say that it looks like my interests have been addressed and I've backed down," she shouted, clearly exasperated with him.

Well, he was getting just as irritated with her. "I

meant that I eliminated the clubhouse because Hopetown doesn't need another banquet facility. You wanted the project smaller. I made it a smaller project. It's called compromise. And it's not the only change I made," he told her, shouting now, too. "I replaced every blasted inch of concrete and macadam with pavers to make the streets, sidewalks and driveways permeable. Do you have a clue what hell that's doing to my profit margin?"

Abby felt desperation as she never had before. She had to get through to him. "Money? That's all you care about! Why can't you forget it? Sometimes I think you're as bent as you say Tracy was. Money didn't make my *parents* happy, did it?"

"Easy for you to say. Your biggest worry financially has been Harley trying to get hold of the vineyard. Remember how that felt? Even if he'd succeeded you all still had somewhere to live. All any of you had to worry about was the upkeep on your family's mansion—*after* you'd all graduated from college without a single school loan. I just finally paid mine off!"

She felt her head would explode. "How I was raised isn't at issue here."

"Really? While you're talking to the reporter, tell her you've remained the most infuriatingly stubborn woman I've ever met. And you can sure as hell tell her you never cut me a break or relaxed your high and mighty standards for a lowly McCarthy."

He stood and looked down at her. "As for worrying

about what people think or not because we're living under your roof, Abby, Jess and I will be moved out within the hour."

Shock reverberated through her. "Where will she stay all day? And what about where she'll sleep?"

"She can sleep and play in that damned shrine my parents left me to deal with. I'll get new mattresses. We'll make do. Construction on the house isn't anywhere near there right now and you'd be shocked by how many peasants live in homes in the middle of renovations."

"Colin, I didn't mean you should move out. She'll be heartbroken to miss the last day of camp. They're having a pizza party."

"So I'll make it up to her. I'll buy her pizza. Just forget us and go back to hiding in your damned tower."

Abby watched in shock as Colin slammed out of her office. She'd never seen him so angry. Not even when he'd arrived, still believing she'd helped to nearly destroy him and his whole family. She blinked back tears. Had she been wrong?

She wouldn't care if she lost the election except that they'd all have to put up with Harley Bryant for four more years, and God only knows how much more damage he'd do in that length of time. There were important issues of public welfare and safety he just kept on ignoring. She knew, for instance, why he was stalling on the federal grant application. Because if the feds came in, they'd force zoning standards on the town that would tie Harley's greedy hands with investors. Look at the way he'd been prepared to smooth over zoning changes and an acreage variance for Colin in exchange for all those mortgage loans. At least the past had come back to bite him.

She'd worked hard to be known as someone who was above reproach and was appalled to be connected with a brewing scandal that called her character into question. But she should have been ready for it. Politics on a small local scale was a lot nastier than she'd realized.

But that was secondary to her losing the election. That could cause real problems for a lot of good people who'd had faith in her. She wanted to win for them, not herself.

A knock on her door sent hope surging through her. Maybe Colin had come back to apologize. She'd be calmer. Try to explain why she'd been so upset.

Abby hated that she was so disappointed when it turned out to be a guest. Before Colin had come back into her life, nothing had been more important than her customers and Cliff Walk.

The guest with the problem was the organizer of the wine club from Ocean City, Maryland. The group had come in on Sunday for the week. With Colin and Jessie there, the group had filled Cliff Walk to capacity.

The Winos, as they called themselves, had decided to leave a day early. There was a hurricane headed north and it was expected to give Virginia and Maryland a glancing blow then head out to sea. There was even speculation that it would downgrade to a tropical storm sometime during the day. Still, they were all worried, so Abby bade them a farewell about an hour and a half later. "Never trust the weatherman," one of them said just before climbing aboard their bus.

As she watched them pull away, Abby realized she'd been so busy helping with luggage and settling their bills that she'd lost track of the time. Colin's truck was gone. She ran up the steps to the second-floor tower room. The door was unlocked and the key sat with a check on top of the television set.

The sitting room was empty.

So was Jessie's room.

He'd even left the little high chair she'd given Jessie for her doll. Abby sat on the bed feeling numb, as if the bottom had dropped out of her world. How could she have become so attached to both of them so quickly?

Cliff Walk was empty but for her. Even Genevieve had gone home and would return only if reservations came in for dinner. Alone and lonely, Abby curled up on the bed, dry eyed and stunned. How could everything change so quickly?

For years her whole world had been these four walls and now she didn't care about anything but a missing drawing board, a discarded gift and their owners.

Abby woke sometime later and wandered to her room. She hadn't slept well last night, because Colin had seemed annoyed that she'd denied him her company. She tried so hard to be above reproach. She worried about even an innocent remark a guest might make while in town about her being in Colin's room. So when he'd asked she'd said no to watching the movie he'd picked up for Jessie when he'd gone to the bank. He'd even casually mentioned the bank appointments, but she hadn't asked what it had been about. That had been their deal. They didn't talk about the Torthúil Gardens project. No wonder he hadn't thought to mention it. He hadn't thought she'd want to know.

And she hadn't.

She rattled around Cliff Walk all day. She cleaned all the rooms. Washed all the bedding. Remade the beds. Once she was finished she put on her favorite classical music and sorted through magazines in the rooms, tossing out the oldest. She arranged books in alphabetical order in the small library in the corner of the parlor. She took a reservation for a room in October, but no one called for dinner. That was unusual for a Friday night. So she left a message for Genevieve on both her home and cell phones that she shouldn't come back.

Still restless, she took a long walk. There was a lot of activity over at the vineyard. Though she was lonely, she also didn't want to talk to anyone, so she walked through the preserve. But that just reminded her of her walks with Colin and Jessie—especially when she came to their meadow.

Everywhere she looked something reminded her of one or the other of them. She worried about Jessie, stuck playing in Tracy's old room all day, but she missed Colin, too. Which was ridiculous since he'd only just be getting back from working on the farmhouse at that time of the day.

She stood at the kitchen counter and picked at some leftovers for dinner, but she wasn't hungry. Finally she just decided to go to bed.

Hopefully she'd be too drained to dream of Colin tonight.

The sound of her mother calling her name dragged Abby groggily out of a restless sleep. She noticed the wind howling as she glanced at the clock. It was one in the morning. Then she heard the rain slapping angrily against the windows. What was her mother doing out in weather like this?

She grabbed her robe and hurried down the stairs, expecting to hear thunder at any moment. It rarely rained like this in the summer unless they were being hit by a thunderstorm. Her mind flashed to the night Colin had arrived with Jessie protected under his slicker. She had to stifle a gasp of pain that sliced through her.

"Mama, what on earth is going on?" she asked when she got halfway down the last flight of stairs. "What are you doing out in this awful weather?"

Juliana stared at her as if she'd lost her mind. "What are you doing asleep? And why didn't you do something with the porch furniture? Sammie, give me the baby and go help Nic and Will get those chairs in here and make sure they get that swing tied down."

Abby turned to see Sam walk out of the parlor

carrying Nikki. Had they all lost their collective minds? "You brought Nikki out in this? At this time of night?" She turned to her mother. "And why would I have brought in the porch furniture?"

"The river's really high already, Abby," said Sammie. "We thought it would be foolish to ride this out at the manor when Cliff Walk will be high and dry until it's time to build an ark."

"Abby, didn't you see the news or the weather forecast since they changed it?" her mother asked.

"I was in bed by eight-thirty, and I didn't turn on a TV or a radio all day."

"One of us should have called you," Juliana fretted.

"Are we getting some of that hurricane?" Abby asked.

"You could say that," Sammie replied, handed off Nikki and went to the door. She opened it as little as she could and slipped out. Even the six inches it had been open left a puddle of rain water in front of the door. Abby just stared. She should mop it up. She wished her head would clear.

"The storm turned and hit Jersey full force. Now it's stalled over Jersey, us and the rest of eastern Pennsylvania. And while it sits it's pumping moisture in off the ocean."

The excess activity in the vineyard made sense suddenly. They'd been trying to get ready.

"They estimate the whole region may get upward of a foot of rain," her mother went on. "Nic went out to check the river then woke us. He's not sure the levee will hold and his retention wall isn't quite finished. We decided it was better to chance the ride up here than stay put."

Abby's blood ran cold. Colin and Jessie were at Torthúil. Were they safe?

Not if the levee failed.

Abby felt paralyzed. She could only stare as her mother went on. "After the thunderstorms this week everything was already pretty soaked. Hopetown and the rest of the towns south of here are in trouble."

"When do they think the river will crest, and how high?" Abby's voice broke.

"It hasn't stopped raining yet," Juliana said. "The storm hasn't even been downgraded to a tropical storm. Perhaps if we get the radio on, we'll get an update." The lights overhead blinked off, then the sconces blinked on. The backup generator had come on.

"I have to warn Colin," she said, and ran into her office. He didn't have a radio. She'd beg him to come back, to get to higher ground. She'd promise to take out a full-page ad telling the entire town to mind their own damned business. Anything to get Colin and Jessie out of harm's way. But when she lifted the receiver the line was dead. She went to the credenza where her cell phone was charging.

"Cell phones don't seem to be working either," Juliana said, following her into the office with Nikki in her arms. "Who are you calling?"

"Colin. He and Jessie moved over to Torthúil." She

snapped her phone shut in frustration. "I have to go warn him."

"Oh, no, you don't. The driveway was in worse shape than we expected. It's practically a stream right now. If the water gets under your tires, you'll go right over the edge. You won't do Colin or Jessie any good if you go over the cliff."

"But, Mama—"

"*No.* We came in Nic's truck. If the eye passes over us he may lend it to you or drive you over there, but otherwise Colin will have to fend for himself. What was he thinking, taking that child there with a hurricane coming?"

"I'm not sure he knew, either." She dropped into the chair behind her desk and dropped her face in her hands. "Oh, Mama, it's all my fault."

"Nothing is ever all one person's fault in a relationship," Juliana said, and settled on the edge of the desk.

Abby stared at the clock. A relationship? Did she and Colin have a relationship? She supposed they did. If not for his plans for Torthúil they'd have a good one. Why had she never thought of that?

Abby felt her mother take her chin. Juliana stared kindly at her. "Tell me," she insisted.

"We had a terrible fight about Colin's project. He's obsessed with making money. It's as if that is the measure of his worth rather than his own character. He's smart, talented, gentle, caring and he's the best parent. But he thinks he has to be a millionaire to protect Jessie."

Abby could see that had her mother confused. But knowing all the facts, Abby did understand. It was just that she knew he was wrong. "Mama, Daddy made Colin leave town all those years ago."

A look of shock crossed Juliana's face. "Your father must have thought he was protecting you. I'd have stopped James if I'd know, but even I was worried. You were a little immature for Colin at the time, and it was obvious how you felt about him. *And* how he felt."

No wonder her father had believed Harley. "But he went too far," Abby said. "He threatened Colin and the McCarthys with taking Torthúil. Their mortgage was late. He said he'd have the bank foreclose if Colin didn't leave and stay gone."

Juliana shook her head slowly, sadly. "He never understood how to use the power he'd been given. All he knew was to use it to get what he wanted. So when Tracy died—"

Abby nodded and finished her mother's thought. "He refused to let Colin come home. And this project is all about making sure no one has that kind of power over him or Jessie ever again."

"So you fought about the project."

"Not just over Torthúil Gardens. The article in the *Courier* implied I had changed sides because I have a relationship with Colin but I was more or less ready for that. I was angry at him because he hadn't told me about the new financing. He couldn't see why I was angry. He gave them ammunition to make me sound like a liar. It could cost me the election. I've worked so hard and they compared me to what—"

"I read the article, Abigail Rose Hopewell. When will you ever stop worrying about the family name?" Juliana smiled kindly. "Where is the difference between Colin caring too much about building wealth and you caring too much about rebuilding what your father damaged? A name is just a name. What is important is who you *are*. And as far as the election is concerned, don't worry about it. Eventually the truth always comes out."

Abby nodded, seeing her mother's wisdom. The truth about the past *had* come out. But she had to wonder how her mother could be so wise when looking at Abby's life and hang-ups and so blind to her own. "If that's true, Mama, why do you care so much about Will's wealth?"

"He lied to me," her mother said stiffly. It had become her automatic response just as hers had about rebuilding the Hopewell reputation.

Why couldn't all this have been this clear to her during her confrontation with Colin? "Will lied because you would have judged him by his bank account and he wanted you to see *him*—to know *him*," Abby told her mother, then reached to touch her shoulder. "Admit it, Mama," she urged with a little squeeze. "Isn't it time to find out who Will really is?"

Juliana stared at her, her eyes wide, rubbing Nikki's back thoughtfully. "That is quite a question. And one I suppose I'd better think over." Her mother tilted her head. "Listen. It sounds as if it's calmed down a bit. I don't like you going down there, but perhaps if we're in the eye of the storm, you can get down and back up before the rains return."

Not wanting to delay further, Abby ran up the steps to get dressed. She didn't care how bad the road was. She had to warn Colin.

Suppose the levee broke. Suppose…

She wouldn't think about it. She'd never wanted to be wrong so badly in her life.

Chapter Fifteen

Colin shoved another piece of Sheetrock into place on the master bedroom wall and began screwing it down. He'd been working nonstop since he'd been sure Jess was fast asleep. The new window air conditioner chugged away, keeping her room cool. It would also do more than double duty, masking the howling wind, the pouring rain that had started less than an hour after he'd put her to bed, as well as the sound of the drill driver.

He hadn't expected the storm to be this intense. The last he'd heard from the group leaving Cliff Walk as he was packing up was that Daniel, a category one hurricane, was expected to be downgraded to a tropical storm within the hour.

All he could think was that it must have come farther north and more inland. He'd know for sure if he'd heard a weather forecast, but his radio had broken the day before, and he'd let Jess watch her portable DVD player while they'd been in the car. It had seemed the least he could do after dragging her out of the camp's wrap party. He was just glad the storm had finally moved on.

He finished yet another section of the wall. When the familiar and strangely soothing whir of the driver trailed off, Colin thought he heard pounding from below. He stopped but heard only silence so he chalked the noise up to exhaustion. And guilt.

Jessie was not happy with him. She missed Abby. Hell, *he* missed Abby. Here he was working on the master bedroom he'd designed with her in mind and she might never speak to him again. He couldn't believe he'd lost his cool that way.

"Way to win her trust, bozo," he lectured himself.

It had been so completely unlike him to lose his temper the way he had. He thought the things he'd said were true, but at the same time he'd wished he'd just shut up and swallowed his anger.

Another series of short thuds vibrated through the house and dragged his attention from his glum thoughts. As he headed down the slightly creaky steps to the first floor, he realized the noise he'd heard was someone pounding on the front door. He didn't have his watch on but it had to be going on two in the morning. His heart leaped at the thought that it might be Abby. Maybe she couldn't sleep, either. He opened the door and his wish was granted when she all but launched herself into his arms. He couldn't apologize fast enough.

"I'm sorry," she cried, at the very same time.

He clutched her to his chest. "I'm sorry too, sweetheart. I had no right to tell you how to react to that article."

She squirmed to get out of his arms and grasped his hand. "None of that matters right now. You have to come back to Cliff Walk with me."

"In the morning. I don't want to wake Jess. She was so grumpy with me all day. And now that you're not so angry at me maybe I can—"

"Colin! You might not be able to get out by morning. Nic went down to the levee. He's worried that our section won't hold. Maybe the rest won't, either."

"The storm's stopped. We'll be fine. You guys really are obsessed with this river thing, Ab."

Her eyes went wide but not with anger. She was really frantic. "Colin, this is a full-blown hurricane. And it's not over. We're in the eye. The worst is coming any minute. You have to get out now!"

Colin shook off his exhaustion and raked a hand through his hair. "I'll get Jess," he said, and pivoted, shouting over his shoulder. "I didn't listen to any weather reports all day."

"Neither did I," she said, following him up the stairs. "Mama arrived at Cliff Walk and woke me. I'd have been here earlier, but she wouldn't let me leave until the eye passed overhead."

"Thank God for that. That driveway can be dangerous in heavy rain." He pushed open Jessie's door and blinked. She wasn't in her bed.

"Where is she?" Abby gasped behind him and flipped on the light.

He rushed to the closet, thinking she might have gotten frightened and taken refuge in there. The closet was empty. "Under the bed," he said, and Abby dropped to her knees.

"No. Colin, she's not here!"

"Maybe she went looking for me," he said, and rushed toward the new master.

"Maybe she's in her new room," Abby shouted, and ran the other way.

He was in a cold sweat by the time he turned around to head back down the hall. Abby had already checked Jessie's new room, so they separated again, each to check another of the original four bedrooms. Abby was in the bathroom, already looking in the tub, when he got there. She shook her head, blinking away tears.

"Downstairs. She has to be downstairs," he said in a shaky voice he could hardly recognize. He'd never felt fear like this. "Jessie! Jess," he shouted, nearly slipping down the stairs. He ran for the addition. Abby was calling frantically now, too, as she moved through the dining room, living room and toward the old kitchen.

They met in the dimly lit family room and stared at

each other. He honestly didn't think he could move. "God, Ab. Did somebody take her?"

"We need to call the police." Abby reached for her cell phone. "No!" she cried, and ran to the French doors. "No service here, either! This can't be happening." She ran a frantic hand through her hair as he checked the one landline he'd put in. It was silent.

"The phones are out at Cliff Walk, too," Abby told him. "And we're on a backup generator for electricity."

As if on cue, the lights went out. "Stay put," he told her. "I put a flashlight next to Jessie's bed."

But when Colin got there it wasn't where he'd put it. He felt around the floor and under the bed but couldn't find it. He'd had one in the master, too, so he found his way as fast as he could down the hall into the unfamiliar room. Once he got his bearings in the pitch darkness, he grabbed his high-powered, combination flashlight-lantern. He yelled to Abby that he'd be right there and stopped by Jessie's room again to get that flashlight for Abby. Two people looking was better than one. But the flashlight wasn't there. Anywhere. Neither was Jessie's backpack or Dog-dog or her baby doll. "Where the hell is she?"

"Colin," Abby shouted. "Colin, I think I see something outside."

He got there a lot quicker with the help of the lantern. Abby still stood staring out the French doors, her hands splayed on the windows. "Jessie?" he asked, incredulous but desperately hoping for the nearly impossible. "I can't imagine Jess going out in a storm or in the dark. But it wasn't raining yet or fully dark when I put her to bed. And she was still so angry with me."

"No. It's not her I see," Abby said, dashing his foolish hope, "but there's something in the grass out there. Look. Off to the right."

He unlocked and opened the doors. With the glass out of his way, he shined the high-intensity beam where Abby pointed. It looked like some sort of cloth. He jumped the four feet to the ground, turned back and took Abby by the waist to lift her down. Once her feet were on the ground, he let go, turned away and ran toward the light-colored lump in the grass some fifty yards away.

Colin fell to the sodden ground on his knees and clutched the pink material in his hands. "It's the blanket we got her for Mary Beth."

He felt Abby's hand on his shoulder. "Was she mad enough at you to try to get to Cliff Walk?"

He stumbled to his feet. His knees had started shaking. Or maybe he'd just noticed. "Jess! Jess!" he shouted.

Abby grabbed him as he headed off to the left toward Cliff Walk. "Colin, I didn't pass her coming here. Neither did Mama and the others. We need to make sure she's not down here near the river before we search for her somewhere else."

What she said made sense. "Right. We need to check here first."

"What about the barn?" Abby asked. "I told her about how Tracy and I hid in the barn. How your mother let Mary worry about us to teach her a lesson."

He stared at her. Could it be this simple? "Did you tell her the lesson?"

"People are more important than—"

Joy surged through him. "Things!" he finished for her. "She wanted to know why we had to leave Cliff Walk. I always tell her the truth. I told her we argued because you didn't want me to build the development." He grabbed Abby's hand and started running toward the barn. "She said people are more important than things. She has to be there. I know how her mind works. She went there to teach me a lesson."

The wind started to blow again before they took their first steps in the direction of the barn, and a heavy rain followed. The eye had moved on. They were soaked in seconds.

They were nearly to the barn when he splashed into four or five inches of swiftly flowing water. The levee wasn't holding. The water got deeper as they went along and he had to steady Abby as it nearly knocked her off her feet. The water started to thin out a little as they went back up the grade to the barn. He prayed the levee would hold a little longer. With any luck they'd get to the barn and back before the water rose any higher.

When they reached the barn, the small access door within the larger one flapped in the wind. Hopefully that meant Jess had opened it but hadn't latched it. He braced the door open while Abby stepped inside. The wind pulled it out of his hand but he grabbed it, dragging it shut behind him to latch it. There was standing water inside, but at least it wasn't flowing as strongly as outside.

The second he got the door secured, Colin heard the most beautiful thing in the world. For the second time in his life the sound of Jess crying gladdened his heart. It was coming from the loft where he'd found Tracy and Abby all those years ago. He splashed across the old barn to the ladder, but the first rung cracked under his weight.

"Jess. You have to climb down to us," he called up to her.

She peered over the edge of the loft. "I'm scared, Daddy. I tried when it got quiet. I can't reach the step."

She was right, of course. He'd seen her scramble up ladders in the past. She could never get back down.

"Maybe the ladder would hold me," Abby said from next to him. "If I can get up there I can hand her down to you."

He nodded. Other than trying to talk Jess into jumping, he didn't have much of a choice. Abby smiled up reassuringly at Jessie and stepped to the side of the second rung. Then, keeping her feet up against the rails where they were strongest, she made her way to the loft—fourteen feet overhead.

Staring after her, unable to breathe, he swore if they got out of this unscathed, he'd never let either one of them out of his sight ever again.

Abby scrambled into the loft and Jessie ran into her outstretched arms. "I want my daddy," she sobbed.

"I know, baby, I know. He's just down there. We'll get you down from here."

"This was a bad idea, Abby," she declared, and her breath caught unevenly. "I never, never going to teach my daddy a lesson ever, ever again. Me and Mary Beth was scared up here even with our new fuzzy friends."

Abby shuddered while being tempted to laugh. She heard Colin snicker and she peered over the edge at him. He'd set the combination lantern-flashlight on the old hay wagon and was beneath them. Even in the dim light she saw in his eyes the look of helpless love his often comical child always inspired.

"I'm going to hand Mary Beth down so we can show Jessie how easy it'll be for you to catch her." Her silent message was, *For God's sake, don't drop the doll.*

She turned to Jessie who knelt in the hay clutching her doll in one arm and Dog-dog in the other. She gave up the doll, but Abby was sure she'd never get that tattered dog out of her arms.

On her belly, Abby leaned over the edge as far as she could and dropped the doll into Colin's waiting arms. Jessie watched solemnly as he set Mary Beth on the wagon seat.

Abby rolled carefully over and sat up, but Jessie was gone. "Jessie where are you?" she called, and knew she sounded a little frantic.

The water lapping at Colin's ankles was getting deeper. Jessie came out of the gloom carrying the missing flashlight and a backpack. Perfect. She could put the backpack on Jessie and tuck the stuffed dog inside. It would give Colin more to grab hold of when she dropped Jessie.

"Come on. Let's get you into your backpack." Jessie handed it to her. "We're going to tuck Dog-dog inside here where she'll stay nice and dry," Abby promised, all but prying the toy out of Jessie's arms.

After she had the pack secured on Jessie, Abby put her on the first rung of the ladder. "Just stand here and I'll hand you down to Daddy," she told the wide-eyed child.

"It's awful far down," Jessie said, clearly scared.

Abby glanced over the edge then looked away, wishing Jessie were wrong. Weren't things supposed to look smaller, shorter, less scary when revisited in adulthood? It certainly wasn't working out that way this time.

"It's not so far that Daddy can't catch you, kitten," he called up.

"Am I in trouble?" Jessie asked, looking over her shoulder at Colin.

"We'll talk about that later. Right now you have to trust us and do exactly what we say. It's important. We'll get you down okay," Colin promised, and Abby swore his voice at that moment would have soothed a charging bull. He really did always tell Jesse the truth, so it was no wonder she seemed to believe him now.

Before she lost any more of her own confidence, Abby rolled to her belly again, next to the ladder and reached for Jessie's hands. "One, two, three," she counted as much for Colin's sake as Jessie's, then she swung his child out into midair.

"Okay. Now," Colin called, and she let go. Coward that she was, Abby closed her eyes and held her breath until she heard him exclaim, "See, I've got you, Jess. Daddy's got you."

Abby was pretty sure that second phrase had been to reassure himself as well as Jessie.

Knowing how quickly the river could change, Abby didn't waste any time but started down the ladder. Without warning the fifth rung came apart under her hand. Abby screamed as she fell backward. But her landing wasn't as rough as she'd expected. Somehow she found herself safe in Colin's arms. They stared into each other's eyes. Something powerful passed between them as they looked at each other. But was it love, or gratitude?

"Daddy caught you, too," Jessie cried from the wagon seat, breaking the spell.

He set her down and the shocking cold water chased all warm thoughts of love and the future from her mind. She promised herself she'd examine that moment in the future just as soon as they handled the problems they faced in the present. They still had to negotiate the wind and rain and the ever-deepening, rushing water. And now that she wasn't thinking of getting Jessie down, she realized the barn was doing an awful lot of groaning.

"We have to get out of here. If I'd thought it would hold, I'd say we'd be safer in here in the wagon but—" Colin looked toward the doors then rushed across the barn. He pushed open the small access door then pulled it shut, returning to the wagon. "I have an idea. It might work if this old thing still rolls," he said, slapping his hand down on the side of the wagon. "If we roll it out the door and keep to this side, it might help keep us from getting knocked over by the water. I bet it's a good six or eight inches deep in the middle by now. Do you think you can help me get it rolling? We just have to get across the spillover and back to the higher ground.

"What about the doors?"

"I've checked this place out. It's in bad shape. Especially those hinges." He scooped Jessie up, tucked the doll inside her backpack and ran a rope he'd found through the straps, tying them together. Then he told her to curl up under the seat, reassuring her that her toys were still tucked in the backpack. She chattered just as if this had turned into a great adventure. Abby noticed Colin did everything he could to foster the idea.

If she ever had children, she'd like a father for them as good as Colin was. Her breath hitched. Who was she kidding? She wanted Colin to *be* their father. It was finally clear to her. There was no man in the world she cared about, trusted or…loved but Colin. There never had been and there never would be.

"The wind should take the doors off if I push them open but I can always help them along," Colin said, grabbing her attention. He pulled an old pry bar down off the wall, then tossed it into the bed of the wagon. Abby shivered, nearly numb. The cold water lapping at her ankles sapped her strength. But there was still nowhere she'd rather be than by his side, battling to get Jessie to safety.

Colin told her to keep her feet next to the wheel so the water couldn't sweep her off her feet. He gave a mighty heave then and the wagon started rolling. Abby gripped the front-wheel spokes and pushed forward then let go to grab the next one that rose to the top of the arc. Inch by inch the old hay wagon rolled toward the doors. Luckily they'd be heading slightly downward again as soon as they cleared the doors. That should help them build enough momentum to clear the deeper water safely.

As Colin had said, once he heaved the big doors open, the one on the left tore off and tumbled toward the river.

"Isn't that enough room for us to get out?" she shouted, squinting her eyes against the bits of hay the wind sent swirling around the barn.

Colin shook his head. "Can't take the chance. The other one might rip loose and hit us while we're next to it. Better to be done with it now." He grabbed the pry bar and helped the right one on its way by prying the lowest two hinges off the door. Then, muscles bulging, Colin pushed all his weight on the door. The wind got behind the door and ripped it off the barn, sending it tumbling out of sight like the other.

This time, though, Colin went down on his face into the torrent outside the barn. Abby let out a yelp but, much as she wanted to help him, she kept hold of the rope attached to Jessie. She knew what he expected of her. She had to keep his child as safe as she could. She had to watch, horrified, as he managed to gain his feet twice only to be knocked down again by the rushing water. Finally, he managed to scramble forward into the barn on his hands and knees then stand. He stumbled to the wagon and fell against the wheel.

"Give me the rope," he panted. He took it and, his chest heaving, turned her around by her shoulders. When he started to loop the rope through her belt, Abby turned to protest, but he shook his head. "Don't argue. I'm not losing either of you," he said as he finished securing the rope to her belt.

There was little she could say to that, so she let him do what he needed to do and took up her position at the front wheel again as he tied the rope around his waist.

"Let's do it," he said from behind her and the wagon started rolling.

Abby put her hands on the wheel and helped it along, trying to brace herself for the wind and rain. The hardest thing was taking a breath and not drawing in the rain with it.

Colin had them going at a good clip as they moved downhill and it was a good thing, because the water at its deepest was a good eight inches deep—more than enough volume to knock a person off their feet. The wagon kept them from being swept away, and stayed pretty solidly on the ground.

It seemed as if she pushed on those wheel spokes forever. The flow kept forcing her feet against the wheel. She picked up more splinters in her hands than she'd had in her entire life. But at last they made it to shallower water. Colin swept Jessie up into his arms then and wrapped the other around Abby, pulling her toward the house.

They were just about there when Abby saw a branch flying across the field coming straight at them. "Colin," she screamed, and fell, pulling on the rope around his waist.

Colin and Jessie hit the ground just as the branch sailed a few feet over their heads. He got up, stared at her for a split second then held out his hand. She accepted his hand and the quick kiss after he pulled her to her feet. They broke eye contact and took off running, slipping and sliding in the churned-up mud around the house.

Nic had driven her there, joking that he had been a speedboat pilot after all and more used to negotiating water than she was. Now that they had to drive in this torrent of rain, she was glad she didn't have to drive his vehicle back.

They got to Colin's truck and he pushed her inside, shoved Jessie into her lap and slammed the door, then ran around the hood and jumped in. He took Jessie, kissed her and twisted his body to buckle her safely in behind Abby. Abby worried that the normally talkative child was so silent.

Colin looked back at Jessie and smiled.

"Is our adventure over and is now when I'm in trouble?" she asked.

Abby wanted to laugh but she was too exhausted.

Colin chuckled. He was apparently too tired to pretend he was angry. "You can't get the puppy I promised you this morning until we move into the house."

"But Daddy you—" She drew in a sharp breath. "Does that mean we're going back to Cliff Walk to stay with Abby?"

Colin took Abby's hand and kissed it, then leaned close and whispered, "I don't know how to thank you. You saved Jessie's life."

"I can't explain it. I just knew you didn't know what was happening with the weather. I had to get to you."

"You did good, Ab." Then he sat back and winked. "You can be in on our adventures anytime you want. Right, Jess? And no extra charge for the mud bath."

Abby looked in the mirror. Her hair was plastered to her head and she had mud smeared on her face and neck, not to mention the rest of her. All she could do was laugh. She didn't look at all like the neat-as-a-pin, collected person she'd been when he'd first shown up at Cliff Walk.

And of course she wasn't—because Colin had blown back into her life and torn her cold sterile existence apart, only to put it back together with the love she'd always dreamed of.

Chapter Sixteen

Colin shook himself awake. Where was Jessie? And Abby? When he saw the empty twin bed next to his, his panic spiked for a moment. Then he noticed the rest of the room and relaxed. They were back at Cliff Walk with Abby's family. She and Jessie were both safe.

And the sun was shining.

Abby had suggested he and Jess take the room they'd first occupied at the B and B in case she had some bad moments during what was left of the night. Apparently, considering his still pounding heart, he was the one having a moment. More than a few of which would stick with him for a good long time.

He grinned now, though, thinking of his indomitable child. They'd thought after the fright of being stranded in the barn, then enduring that perilous trek to the truck and the more than scary ride up the steep driveway, she might be subdued or fearful. Once inside Cliff Walk, however, she'd chattered excitedly, revealing details of the adventure he'd rather not have shared with Abby's mother.

Dawn had been lightening the sky by the time they'd washed off the mud and gotten to bed but, tired as he was, he knew he'd never get back to sleep now. There seemed to be an unusual buzz of activity outside. Besides, he wanted to know the extent of the damage.

Even though he was still dead tired, Colin stumbled to his feet, aching in places he hadn't known existed. He looked out the window and, through the trees, saw a bunch of people erecting a big tent with a red cross on it.

He dressed quickly and nearly got punched in the nose by Abby when he pulled the door open. "Whoa!" He stepped back and caught her by her shoulders as she stumbled through the door. Colin felt the familiar zing shoot through him that touching her almost always caused.

"Oh, good. You're awake. I was about to knock. Don't worry about Jessie, she's over at Caro's. All the kids are." She had an armful of sheets and went to the bed where Jess had slept, dumping them on the luggage rack at the foot. In full dynamo mode, she started pulling the bed apart. "I hope you don't mind but I'm moving you guys back into the tower suite. It settled Jessie down. She was still worried about going back to the farmhouse. And she wanted to know if she could still have the high chair."

He winced. "I was really—"

"Forget it. It's hers and she knows it now."

He didn't care about any of that. He moved to the other side of the bed and helped her finish. "Did you get any sleep at all?" he asked, concerned that she looked a little pale.

"I slept last night before Mama and the others arrived, remember?"

"Still, you should have rested and you should have woken me if Jess was a problem."

"I only let you sleep for a few hours." She smoothed the bedspread with a practiced hand. "And unless she's hiding in a barn that's about to take a ride down the river, I'd never consider her a problem. Why don't we get Genevieve to feed you then—"

He saluted her. "Aye-aye, captain."

She blinked as if coming to her senses. "I was dictating. Sorry. I've been doing that to everyone all morning. It's just that there's so much to do." Then she looked just plain miserable. "And you don't even know what's going on."

"I'm guessing it has something to do with that huge tent."

She nodded. "Once the storm passed, cell communication came back up. Mama offered our facilities to the Red Cross and we've put out the word that anyone is welcome. Mamma, Nic and Will are setting up cots at Bella Villa. Caroline's husband, Trey, is a doctor—

he's seeing to any injuries, of course. Sam's tending the grapes and I'm putting the elderly in real beds inside Cliff Walk. That's why I was about to wake you. I need this room for the Schroder sisters. They own that red-and-green cottage just south of the manor."

Colin frowned. "That's still relatively high ground there."

Abby looked uncomfortable. "Yes. Well, as I said, they're older. I'd better get a move on."

He stopped her. Something wasn't right. "Spill it. What's happening?"

She looked so…guilty. "I wanted you to eat first. You've got time. They're not expecting the river to crest until four o'clock today."

"There's an *and* in there," he prompted.

She huffed out a breath. "It's predicted to crest at thirty-three point five. That's thirteen and a half feet above flood stage in town."

He ran that figure through his mind and a hand through his hair. He'd grown up here so the layout of the town was engraved on his brain. "That's water nine feet deep in the middle of Main Street. And it's awfully close to topping the levees." Torthúil's levee had already partially failed. "And you let me sleep?"

She put her hand on his arm. "Colin, it's only eight o'clock. Three of your guys heard what was happening up here. They managed to get to Torthúil before River Road flooded. They brought heavy equipment.

Will says they're bulldozing and packing dirt against the levee where it failed."

"I'd better get over there. How is it at the manor?"

She looked worried so he took her hand. "Volunteers are sandbagging the levee for us," she told him. She blinked back tears and gripped his hand. "Please grab something to eat first. We'll keep Jessie safe and out of trouble and then I'll see you later."

The rest of the day went much the same way. He got to Torthúil, thanked his guys for their help. They were doing all that could be done with the equipment they'd brought. They'd added to the levee's height, too, so he suggested they add the weight of the fieldstone to reinforce what they'd already done, and they began handling that. If the house was still there after tonight it would be worth the trouble to gather it all up later. He went to the master suite to collect his tools—just in case the repair didn't hold.

He glanced out the French doors and the scene in the distance pulled him over there. The barn lay in ruins. Over the howling wind that morning, he'd thought he'd heard cracking timbers as he was getting into his truck. He'd been right. His praise of Abby hadn't been overblown. If Jessie had still been in there, she'd have been killed. It was a sobering thought in the midst of an increasingly sobering day.

His plans had to change. There was no question of that now, no matter what the corps of engineers had told him. No matter how much smaller he made the development, Torthúil would still be on a floodplain.

This was a problem he couldn't fix with pavers, stacked housing or eliminating ranch homes. Even if there was never another storm like this one, there was no way he would add even one drop of water to that river. Money just wasn't worth ruined lives. Abby had always known that. Now he understood what she'd been saying. Nothing was worth the chance of hurting someone else.

He turned away from the window and went to collect his tools and Tracy's fantasy collection. For all he knew, by five o'clock that afternoon, those fairies and dragons and one faded castle poster would be all he had left of his heritage to give Jessie. But he'd still have the memories. He'd still have Jess, thanks to Abby. And he still owned a company that could support him and his family.

He went back up to the vineyard to help with the displaced citizens who lived along the river, occasionally catching a glimpse of Abby as she saw to various tasks.

As noon approached, he went over to the manor to help with the sandbagging and to take lunch to Nic, Will and the volunteers. They ran out of sandbags but the river steadily rose. Retreating before the power of nature, they all turned their attention to the manor itself. They decided to move as many of the antiques and family keepsakes as they could to the upper floors—just in case. He didn't think he was the only one praying they were wasting their time.

The first floor was cleared by four and the volunteers left for the vineyard, deciding to watch from high ground to see if their efforts had been successful. Colin, with Nic and Will, stood ready to run but as they watched, the river rose to lap only a foot below the top of the levee. All the while they knew that downstream nothing could help Hopetown. It had been flooding for hours already. There was no question he'd help with the cleanup, but he wanted to do more. They all did.

He went back to the vineyard and helped Abby and the Red Cross workers serve dinner. They walked hand in hand after that to Caro and Trey's to pick up Jess. Abby was tired and frustrated. Her friends were in trouble in town and she was cut off from helping because the roads and bridges were flooded out.

They didn't talk about their relationship but about the storm damage to the vines and to the trees and pathways on the preserve. For his part, he didn't bring it up because it seemed insensitive and wrong when so many people were suffering. He didn't bother to tell her about scrapping the project, because it really changed nothing between them except to remove an excuse to argue.

Their problems were about more than his now-defunct plans. There was no question in his mind that he loved her and wanted a life with her. After last night he couldn't believe she didn't love him. He just didn't know if she'd be willing to trust in that love, trust in herself because their love came wrapped in the passion she'd learned to fear. Which put him back where he'd started.

How did he convince her to trust her heart? To trust him?

He honestly didn't know.

Genevieve's words returned to the forefront of his mind. *Find the one thing you can give her that no one else can.*

Colin had convinced himself *the one thing* was to give up the development. But he'd refused to try because he'd wanted so desperately to succeed. He'd even tried to convince himself he could give her Jessie, the child he could see she was coming to love. She'd come to love Jess so much that after he'd yanked her away, Abby had put her life in danger to save his child. And she'd saved him from that flying branch, too, but he still wasn't sure of her love for him, because he'd been wrong about both of those paths to her heart.

Sam had told him exactly what he needed to do, but he'd been too blinded by surface issues to see it.

The only way to show Abby his love was to love her no matter what. Unconditionally. And he hadn't done that.

He'd gotten selfish.

He'd gotten angry.

He'd tried to change her. He'd tried to make her into someone who could put her happiness before the people she cared about. So what if she cared what people said about her? Hopetown was her home. She had friends here whose opinion of her she valued. Townspeople she was trying to win over so she could replace Harley Bryant as mayor—for *their* good, not her own.

Other than Jess, Abby was the only person in Hopetown whose opinion mattered to him. And he'd be a liar if he said he didn't want her to be proud of him. Luckily he finally understood in his heart what she'd been saying all along. Abby measured worth by a person's character, not dollar signs.

That was the way he'd been raised to think, too. He'd forgotten that in his drive toward wealth and power but luckily he'd remembered in time.

In time to help Hopetown.

In time to show Abby her heart would be safe with him.

Chapter Seventeen

The morning after the river crested, Abby stared down from the terrace behind Cliff Walk. The river had finally receded. An hour later, the Red Cross transport headed into town full of volunteers. She went with Nic while Colin drove with his men and the heavy equipment. When they got there she saw he was clearly appalled by the destruction the river had left in its wake.

Along Main Street, the town was in a shambles. The high-water mark was a foot into the second story of every structure on the river side of Main Street, and to the top of the first story on the other side.

The river didn't just rise. It swept along almost angrily, as if punishing the places it wasn't normally allowed. It tore things apart and it carried debris with it that crashed through windows and knocked downspouts, light fixtures and signs off buildings.

But there was something incredibly good going on there on that awful day. All the business owners were helping each other. And the residents who'd escaped the flood were out helping, too. She was proud to show Colin this side of her town. *Their* town.

"Your mother told me the first day I was back that the spirit of town had changed drastically. There really aren't strict class structures the way there were when I was young. I'm glad," he said then got down to work.

Everywhere she went all day she either saw him working, or organizing, or she heard people talking about him and his men and how much help they were. At one point, she introduced him to Harry Clark and pointed out the badly damaged biker shop as Harry trudged inside to get back to his cleaning.

"That's one of the people you were sitting with at the zoning meeting," Colin said. "So your friend owns a biker shop. What other interesting things am I going to find out about you, Ms. Hopewell?"

She'd grinned and whispered in his ear, "That's my secret."

He'd apparently stayed to help Harry until his men came to get him to tackle a bigger problem. They'd gotten involved at the far end of town, pumping out the underground garage of the condo buildings that sat right on the riverbank. The condos were only three years old and were supposed to be a modern interpretation of the clapboard homes so prevalent in the area. Abby thought they were just plain ugly.

News of the flooding had spread like wildfire. Word was that the engineers from the Pennsylvania Emergency Management Agency had their hands full all over the state and couldn't get there before the next day. The condos built by Harley Bryant's brother-in-law had taken a real hit. Even though they'd been touted as floodproof, Colin's men thought they were unsafe. The fire chief had wanted to know what Colin, a licensed architect, thought so he could make the call on whether it was safe to let the residents back in or not.

Abby arrived at the first condo as Colin walked up from its underground garage. He wore a yellow hard hat that he took off and tossed to one of his guys. He spoke first to the chief, then to the head of the condo association. They talked for several minutes, then they shook hands and Colin walked away. He saw Abby and headed her way.

"What's up with the condo building?" she asked.

Colin frowned. "It's a death trap. The river undermined the foundation."

"Oh, Colin. Can they go back in to get their things?"

He shook his head as he had when talking to Chief Anders. "It just isn't safe. And I wouldn't count on the stability of the second building even if we get the lower level pumped out by the end of the day." He hooked his thumbs in his waistband and shook his head after a tired sigh. "I don't know how Harley's brother-in-law could claim they were floodproof. I promised to try to come up with a solution for the owners after the emergency is over. It won't be cheap but at least the association has flood insurance."

She grimaced, thinking of all the people who owned a piece of the hideous things. Colin looked so tired and dispirited that Abby tried to lighten the moment. "Any way to make them less ugly?"

He looked over his shoulder, chuckled and said, "I'm not a miracle worker, sweetheart."

Then one of his men called out for help on the crumbling foundation of one of the oldest buildings in town. She tiptoed and kissed him on the cheek then heard someone call her name now, too. "See you later," she said, and stepped back to watch him go off to lend assistance.

Abby stood, watching Colin with pride as he crouched down next to jeweler Scott Timmons to look at the foundation of his shop. If there was a problem with it, she hoped and prayed there was some way Colin could save the building that had once housed Hopetown's first library.

Abby heard her name called and reluctantly turned away from the drama unfolding at river's edge, only to face Madeline Booker, the reporter who'd written the article that had caused her argument with Colin.

She charged up to Abby. "Miss Hopewell. Are you reevaluating your stance on Colin McCarthy's project yet again, considering this new flood?"

"I'm not aware that I ever reevaluated it in the first place. I've said repeatedly that all permits for any new building should be refused. That hasn't changed. You really should have called me to check out your story. Harley Bryant isn't a very reliable source."

"Then you're denying a romantic relationship with McCarthy."

Abby tilted her head and smiled, realizing she'd kissed Colin in front of the whole town and hadn't thought a thing of it or what anyone thought. She especially didn't care what Madeline Booker thought. She'd just done what felt right and it felt good. Really good. "I'm not denying it at all."

Booker took a short step back, clearly nonplussed. "Well...so...you're confirming a relationship as Mayor Bryant claims."

Abby smiled. "And you just confirmed Harley as your source." Booker frowned but remained silent. "I'd be careful whose *truths* you print from now on," Abby cautioned. "And as I said, I never changed my mind about Torthúil Gardens. Colin and I have simply agreed to disagree."

"You really think you can remain impartial?"

Abby shot her a jaundiced look. "It's called integrity, Ms. Booker. I'm in the mayoral race for the good of the town."

"But the mayor seems to feel McCarthy isn't all that interested in the good of the town. How do you justify that in your mind and heart?"

"I justify it because Colin is a good man. After I explained about the runoff problem, he altered his plans considerably, using permeable paving techniques, changing the scope of the project and more. I don't know what he'll do now. You should ask him. And maybe you should also ask when he started looking for his new financing. It was just after the zoning meeting."

"You said you're in the mayoral race for the good of the town. Isn't it really about the two leading families battling for power?"

"You mean the Bryants and the Hopewells? I like to think there are still those of us who do it in spite of that. I came here to help my fellow citizens today, and my reason for wanting to be mayor is no different. We have problems, and I believe I can solve them better than Harley Bryant. At the zoning meeting in July, he called the spring flood 'Main Street's little water problem' just before he tabled discussion of the federal grant money we need to help fix this." Abby gestured at the muck and silt still to be cleaned up and to the low-lying area nearest to the river where the water still swirled. "Does this look like a little water problem to you?"

Madeline Booker frowned, then she glanced over at Colin. Abby followed the reporter's gaze to where Colin stood knee-deep in water, drawing on the side of the building, his men and several others looking on. She smiled when the men all nodded. It seemed Colin had come up with a plan to save the building.

When she looked back at Madeline, the reporter had turned in the other direction and was now gazing up Payton Street, where Harley stood in his summer best circled by TV cameras and microphones.

The woman looked back at Abby and let her eyes travel down from her slipping ponytail to mud-soaked jeans then on to her muddy sneakers. The difference between them was staggering. Abby chuckled. "I think you can see the voters will have no problem choosing between our varying styles."

"I'm sure you know my paper was about to endorse him. My editor isn't going to be happy if I print a retraction," she muttered, looking troubled.

Abby couldn't help sharing what she'd only learned in the wee hours of that morning. "Worrying about appearances isn't worth the things we lose, Ms. Booker."

As darkness fell on the town, Abby and Colin hitched a ride back to Cliff Walk with Nic. Colin had no sooner climbed in and put his arm around her than she started to drift off with her head on his shoulder. As she surrendered to sleep, Abby drank in the secure feeling of being in his arms.

The absence of movement woke her sometime later. She opened her eyes and looked up at Colin. For a long moment she just gazed up at his handsome face, waiting for her foggy brain to kick into gear.

"We're home," he whispered finally, and smoothed a hand over her hair, smiling gently.

Abby smiled, feeling cherished. For the first time in nine years she knew she could trust a man—this man—with her heart. With her body. With everything she was.

"We should go inside," Colin said in an almost

hushed tone, as if not wanting to break the mellow mood inside the vehicle. "And Nic better get over to Caro's before he falls asleep."

Abby sat up but Nic, who was slumped down in the seat with his head resting on the headrest, said, "Too late. Nic is already asleep and may pass the night right here."

Colin chuckled and opened his door, flooding the truck's cab with light. Nic groaned and sat up. "I'm going. I will bring Jessie back in the morning."

Abby slid to the ground after Colin and found herself engulfed in his arms. The truck moved away from in front of Cliff Walk as Colin dipped his head and touched his lips to hers. Pulling her tighter against him, he deepened the kiss and she sighed, happy to grant him entrance.

She'd thought before when they'd kissed that he'd tasted dark and dangerous, but now she saw and felt with a different heart. He was exciting and just a bit mysterious. But that was because he had the potential to take her places she'd never had the nerve to dream of going.

Abby was no longer afraid to dream or take the journey. As long as she took it with him.

"I missed you today," he whispered against her lips, his fingers spearing into her hair. Electricity shot down her spine, awakening a hunger she knew only Colin could satisfy.

"We saw each other today a few times," she told him, trying to focus but finding coherent thought all but impossible. How could just the touching of fully clothed bodies do this to a perfectly organized mind?

"But we didn't see each other like this," he argued. "Awful as it was being out in the storm, at least we were together. Was it only yesterday we were fighting that storm together?"

"Very early yesterday but, yeah," she agreed, "it feels like it happened ages ago. We haven't had nearly enough time together since. We should remedy that," she suggested, and squirmed a little closer. There was no mistaking his arousal.

"But you're dead on your feet," he said, and let go of her with one arm and turned toward the house with the other still holding her waist.

She smiled, remembering the last time she'd managed to get past his reserve and good intentions. It was a long time ago. Too long.

Lights blazed inside Cliff Walk. The old house was full to bursting with elderly residents from all over Hopetown, and Abby didn't care who saw them walking arm in arm.

How supremely liberating!

But their presence did complicate things a bit. She still wanted time alone with Colin. Which meant she had to get him all the way to the third floor.

They left their muddy shoes and socks on the porch and padded quietly into the foyer and up the stairs.

Outside the door to the second-floor tower suite and across from the door to her private stairway, Abby managed to stand on tiptoe and nip his ear. Colin stopped dead and whipped her around in his arms. She found herself pinned against the stairway door.

"The last time you did that, you were eighteen and I warned you not to push me. I'm a lot more deprived these days. And I've been wanting you from a lot closer proximity for weeks. I could have lost you in that storm. I have—" he broke off and kissed her…hard "—much, much less control tonight!"

This time she didn't even try to hide her grin. One kiss was all it had taken that night. "Good. I'm too tired to have to work very long at this." She pressed her pelvis more firmly against his. "And speaking of hard," she breathed into his ear.

He growled and his mouth took hers in a kiss that had her ready to crawl out of her own body into his. He devoured her lips, tasted every square inch of her mouth, held her so tight she had trouble drawing a breath.

Or was that just because his nearness took her breath away?

Then he let go. Stepped back, his chest heaving.

She looked up into his burning gaze and knew she'd built the fire. She also knew he was holding on to his control by a thread.

Abby felt powerful. She'd felt it once before, but this time she understood it was a power he'd given her. His need. His desire. His heart was in her hands.

She moved toward him, but he held up his hand—his key, looped over his finger, dangled across his palm. "Am *I* using mine? Or are *we* using yours? It's your call but there's no going back."

Abby grinned and turned to push her key into the lock, then pulled the door open. She looked back over her shoulder at him and notched her chin up. "Follow me."

"Anytime, anywhere," he whispered close behind her. "I'll never let you out of my sight again."

It was Abby's turn to shiver in delight at his bold promise. Because if she'd learned one thing, it was that Colin McCarthy always kept his promises.

Chapter Eighteen

Colin scooped Abby into his arms and carried her up the narrow steps.

He'd let her break his control nine years ago and again just now, but this was as far as he'd let her go. From here on, this was his seduction. This time he'd be in control.

For as long as he could hold on anyway.

He walked up the last step and into a sitting room. And it so personified Abby it took his breath away. The sitting room was done in rich burgundy and gold with a comfy upholstered loveseat and chaise. The tower room to the other side used the same colors in an imposing Victorian conopy bed draped in gauzy fabrics and silk wall coverings. He carried her to the bathroom, nudged the door open and maneuvered them in as smoothly as he could. There was a modern double-wide shower stall, a claw-foot tub and an old dresser turned into a sink base.

He set her down in front of the shower, reached in and twisted on the spray. Then he settled his mouth over hers again, needing the taste of her like some narcotic. Good thing she wasn't illegal. And after tonight she'd be all his.

He found the hem of her shirt and pushed his hands underneath, moving it and his hand north while he continued to drink his fill of her sweet mouth. The feel of her skin and the noise she made in the back of her throat pushed his need higher.

He had to give up her lips to get the shirt over her head. The sight of Abby's perfect breasts hiding behind the silky bra nearly took him to his knees in pure worship of her beauty. He skimmed his hands inside her cotton shorts and over her nicely rounded bottom, feeling the skimpy panties that would soon be all that stood between him and nirvana.

He left her mouth and kissed her neck then let his lips travel over her soft skin to her breasts, cupping their perfection and laving first one nipple then the other through the sheer cups of her bra. She moaned. It was a seductive sound.

He dropped to his knees and pulled the shorts with him, then he ran his hands up the back of her impossibly long legs, kissing her silky thighs then the black nest of curls at their juncture. Her knees buckled and he knew he'd pushed her as far as he could until they made it to that decadent bed of hers.

Colin looked up at her, horrified to see tears streaming down her cheeks. He stood and cupped her face. "Abby, honey. What—"

She covered his mouth with her fingertips. "I love you, Colin McCarthy," she choked out. "You make me feel so amazing. And I'm not afraid of that anymore. I can't tell you how wonderful it feels to have you touch me and know this is right. That I can trust you. That I can trust me."

He grinned and kissed away her tears, then shrugged out of his shirt. Unbuckled his belt. Fished his wallet out of his pants before dropping them in a heap. He tossed the wallet onto the sink base before turning his attention back to Abby.

"You want to help?" he asked, noting a little frown line form between her eyebrows.

"Um, yeah." She hesitated, seemed to screw up her courage and stepped right up to him. And when she leaned against him, he couldn't stifle a groan. The heat of her body seemed to envelop his barely clothed arousal. Her soft hands moved a little hesitantly over his ribs then downward. She slid her slightly clumsy hands inside his briefs and across his butt. He really thought he could take anything she dished out, but then her mouth landed on his nipple and her beautiful white teeth scraped over it they way he'd done to her.

He was a beaten man.

He reached for her shoulders and pulled the straps

of her bra down before quickly unhooking it. Just as quickly as he could, he stripped off both their bottoms. "We're wasting water," he said, his voice hoarse with need and mounting tension.

She tilted her head and grinned brazenly. "Seems to me we're wasting time."

Colin shook his head. "Oh, no, we aren't," he promised. Stepping inside and under the spray, he pulled her in with him. He turned her back to him—the better to wash her hair, the better to keep his hands off temptation.

Then he made the mistake of looking down at her bottom, inches from his arousal. Before he took her against the hard shower wall, he hooked his arm around her, took her hand and plunked the shampoo into it.

Colin grabbed the bar of soap and the back brush, then he scrubbed himself. Fast. Soaped up his hair and rinsed off. Then he turned to find her watching him.

"That was quick. I guess you aren't wasting time or water after all," she said, all saucy and perky.

And just that quickly, he realized what had happened. Sometime in the past day, he'd found the Abby he'd lost. She really wasn't afraid anymore. She could have given him no greater gift.

Rubbing the soap between his hands, he built up a good lather and reached for her. He spread the slippery foam over her fine-boned shoulders, across her long lean back, then forward over her ribs and her breasts. He knelt, grabbing the soap, lathering up again, then he lavished attention on her slender legs, ending with the curls guarding the secrets he intended to discover for himself once again.

Abby cried out—a sound he relished—when his fingers slid through that magical cleft. And Colin's patience snapped once again, for the final time. He stood and grabbed the sprayer, rinsed them both off. He meant to grab a towel but Abby put her arms around his neck and kissed him. This time her tongue sought his. Her body seemed to worship his. She pushed him backward and his calves met a bench he hadn't noticed before. He dropped down and she straddled him. "Colin, I can't wait anymore. I want you now."

Colin took her at her word but refused to do more than love her with his hands and mouth. She protested at first but pretty quickly she didn't have anything to complain about.

He toweled them off when she was limp and satisfied, carried her to the bed and nearly followed her down—but there was one more thing he wanted to do first. He wasn't done with her. But he wasn't taking any chances on losing her again. This time there'd be no misunderstandings.

Abby wanted to feel Colin's arms around her. She tried to pull him down next to her, but he shook his head. It wasn't fair. She'd had all the pleasure. Need and tension were carved on his features. She couldn't let him leave, but then she stopped worrying.

"Oh, I'm not done with you," he said, once again seemingly able to read her mind.

Funny that didn't bother her in the least anymore, either. In fact, she kind of liked it! She put her arms up again but he took her hands.

"But I'm not skipping this part." He was so incredibly aroused she could hear it in his deepened voice. The pupils of his eyes had swallowed the blue and the pulse under her fingertips thundered. But he looked solemn and determined, too.

What could be so important? Then the growing seriousness in his gaze held her captive. "I love you, Abby," he said softly. "And I want a lifetime with you. Not just a night. I want children with you. And I want to raise them at Torthúil. I've been renovating that house for *you*. I hoped that's something you'd want. Oh, God, please tell me that's what you'd want."

Abby blinked back happy tears. She tried to tell him she'd like nothing better, but nothing came out when she opened her mouth. It didn't matter, because he turned away to grab his wallet. She thought he'd gone after a condom, but when he turned back and opened his palm, lying in the center was a square-cut diamond, the band and setting encrusted with sweet tiny diamonds. It looked antique but she knew where he'd gotten it. Scott Timmons. She'd admired the ring when he'd shown it to her after he'd designed it.

"I thought Scott would have to stay closed for a pretty long time."

Colin grinned. "We bartered. I'm fixing the foundation. He steered me toward this. He says it's one of a kind. Just like the lady I wanted it for. Only one problem. This may be all over town by morning." He picked up her left hand and kissed the back of it. "It's still a small town." He kissed each knuckle. "I'm going to be one embarrassed guy if you turn me down." He turned her hand over and kissed the palm. "I came back with the dream of building Torthùil Gardens. That isn't going to happen now, but it doesn't matter. Because I have a new dream. You."

"Oh, Colin, I'm sorry about the project. But I know you'll build something just as wonderful someplace else." She sat up to kiss him.

"I'd be proud to be your wife. I'm proud of you. You were wonderful today. You helped so many people. If someone doesn't like it, they can…well, they can just go jump in the damn river."

Colin chuckled and lifted her hand to slide the ring on. Then he kissed her and they fell to the bed. He moved over her and started the magic all over again, kissing and suckling every inch of her.

Abby barely got to touch him at all because the tension built faster this time, and he took her higher. And higher.

Then he finally listened when she begged him to stop the torture and he settled between her thighs. Just before he entered her, he told her one more time how much he loved her.

Just the way he'd promised.

Epilogue

Camera in hand, Colin slipped up behind Abby and snapped several shots. She was a picture standing on the wrought-iron balcony in her frothy wedding dress, her midnight-dark hair dressed in pearls and satin ribbons. All day she'd stolen his breath every time he looked at her.

"Have you ever seen anything so beautiful as our wedding?" she asked, looking over her shoulder at him.

He snapped one more photo and placed the camera on the bench at the foot of the bed. Then he walked out onto the balcony to wrap his arms around her and gaze out over the river, her silky hair brushing his cheek. "Actually, it all sort of pales in comparison to the bride."

She tilted her head back and smiled up at him.

"Flattery will get you just about anything, handsome. But really," she said, and squeezed his hands where they rested at her waist. "Tracy's garden is just so perfect. It was a stroke of genius to lease the farmland to the town and turn it into a community garden. She'd have loved it."

Colin took a breath and inhaled her sweet mint and lavender scent. "I think you're right," he said against her ear before dropping a kiss on her bare shoulder.

"Aren't you glad we waited to be married there? I felt almost like she was with us. It was sweet that so many people from Hopetown showed up for the ceremony, too."

"They wanted to cheer for their mayor."

"They were there for you, too. It was your idea to dredge the river. It'll probably save the town. I just applied for the grant money. And I wouldn't have gotten into office in time to do it if you hadn't gotten Harley and his brothers-in-law arrested for cutting corners on those ugly condos."

"Hey!" he protested, and nipped at her ear.

Abby chuckled and shivered at the same time. "Okay, *previously* ugly condos. I just can't believe none of us remembered Harley had appointed his other brother-in-law as building inspector."

"Well, at least they all went to prison. I love a happy ending."

"And speaking of happy endings, you never told me how you feel about the announcement your mother made after she caught your bouquet?"

She turned in his arms and tilted her head as she gazed up at him a thoughtfully. "I'm thrilled Will finally got Mama's promise to marry him. And our kids will have a grandfather now."

Colin nuzzled her neck. He moved on to her jaw as his fingers started working on the long row of buttons down her back. When the dress was undone but for one strategic last button, he scooped her up in his arms then stood her next to the bed.

"Speaking of promises," he whispered against her lips, slipping the last pearl button through its loop. "I made one to Jessie. She wants a baby brother or sister as soon as possible."

Abby smiled, her green eyes sparkling. She tunneled her fingers in his hair as her dress fell to the floor in a puddle of satin and lace. It had been pretty but nowhere near as breathtaking as the woman beneath. "Well, then I guess for Jessie's sake, we'd better get working on it."

Colin stepped back and gazed at his lovely bride. "Oh, yeah," he said with a loving smile. "All for Jessie's sake."

* * * * *